TAMING THE MONSTER

BLACKWOOD ACADEMY BOOK 3

K.J. THOMAS

Editor: Samantha Wiley

Proofreader: Rachel

Cover Artist: Thomas Moore Jr.

❀ Created with Vellum

To my dark and twisted readers:
Never stop being you...

CHAPTER 1

ASHER

6 months later

The amount of glass that's on the floor in this eerie and dark house is utterly shocking. No one can walk anywhere without feeling the crunch of the skin piercing glass under their shoes.

It's been a while but it's time for all of us to move forward. Ever since that fateful day six months ago, nobody has stepped foot back into the Stone's house, not even the Stones. In all honesty, how can we get back to our normal lives when we just went through hell?

Vito, Mac and I have ten guards in case there is any other problems as we enter Avery's old house to check it out. We also brought a cleaning crew to get rid of any evidence from that day.

At first the windows were boarded up. This is a nice

neighborhood and of course the people started complaining to the HOA, so we hired men to come in and install new windows, but left the rest of the house just sitting the way it was.

I'm not sure why we boarded the house up, maybe it's because Arya and Garrett wanted it that way. I take in a deep breath and will away the dark and depressing thoughts. That's all I need is for my men to see me shed a tear or two. I can only imagine what would happen, I would never live this down.

"It could be worse," Vito says as he walks up behind me. I had to take a deep breath, as I wanted to shout, the fucker scared the shit out of me. Maybe it's because of who he is, he's able to sneak up on people like a stealthy rabbit on crack.

He smiles at me with a twinkle in his eye, he knows exactly what he did. Vito and I have grown a lot closer in the last six months than I would've ever imagined. He's the father/grandfather figure I've never had and I'm enjoying every minute of it. In our world you never know when things can change, when shit can go sideways.

It's just nice having someone to look up to. For years I had no one. I'm nineteen-years old and in charge of the East Coast. Vito explained that he doesn't want to venture out past Chicago, he's very happy where he is.

That makes me feel better seeing how we'd be going to war if he wanted more. I believe he's doing it for his granddaughter. Having more power and prestige comes with a lot more money and recognition, I guess. His granddaughter will always be taken care of. I take another deep breath. This time, it didn't go exactly how I wanted it to.

I've got to get out of this funk. I look up and notice Vito watching me. It all makes sense now. We're here because of what happened, and for some reason I'm not able to move on. It's severely hard because things hit so close to home. *Avery almost died again.*

This shit has happened to all of us before but this time it was different, things mean a helluva lot more to me now than they did then.

I walk over to the kitchen island and use my hand to get rid of dust, shards of glass and clumps of dirt.

This is the spot that Avery liked to sit all the time. As soon as I make sure that the chair's clean enough, I hop up on it. I watch everybody as I take in the scene. Besides me and Vito, Mac was the one that's been impacted the most. The sadness hasn't left his face for so long. He lost a lot of good people that were close to him that day.

My mind wanders back, I remember almost every detail of that day. Maybe this is what I needed to do, to let go. I need to relive it one more time.

I'll never be able to pinpoint exactly what woke me up that night. It could have been a strange noise or a feeling. Something forced me out of bed.

The voices of laughter carry up all the way from the

kitchen to our room. Normally I'm a deep sleeper, but something else happened. Nothing seems to be out of the ordinary and nobody seems to be in danger.

I could walk down like this, but I don't think all the guys will appreciate seeing my junk. I get out of bed and find a pair of basketball shorts I wore the other day.

I take my time walking toward the kitchen, looking at the Stone's house and listening to Avery laugh along with the other guys. Nothing makes me feel better than hearing that my girl's happy.

As I reached the top of the stairs and make my way down, everyone grows quieter. Not because they noticed I was coming, something else. I walk a little faster trying to find Avery. I don't have a good feeling.

I don't have to wait long, as soon as I come down halfway she's standing right there in front of me, with a big smile plastered on her face. This girl's my world. Everywhere she goes she has a magnetic pull, people navigate toward her. Even all the damn guards love her.

Noticing Avery is heading toward the stairs, I reach out my hand so she can grab it. I can pull her up the rest of the stairs to meet me halfway, then we can go back to bed together. I give her a smirk letting her know what I'm thinking.

At the same time she looks at me, is the same time everything shifts. I can't process what I'm seeing. I'm seeing it, but it's making no sense to me right now. By the time it does make sense, it might be too late.

"Avery, get down!" I start screaming with everything I can. Avery froze, she is in shock and staring at me.

Mac and about five of the other guards come running out into the foyer to see what's going on. They notice my frantic state and must know something is horribly wrong. All of them freeze in their tracks and start to glance between me and Avery. This whole thing lasted about ten seconds. That's when I got my ass in gear. I jump off the remaining eight or nine steps. Not the best idea, but I can get there faster if I jump.

Mac picks up on what's going on fast. He screams in panic at Avery, too. All the guards start running in her direction.

"Avery, get down."

"Run!"

"Your shirt."

"Avery."

"Avery, run."

Her mouth is open wide as she looks back and forth between everybody that's yelling at her.

From what seemed to take minutes, was most likely only seconds. All of us were able to get to her.

As soon as we reach her that's when the sounds of glass exploding starts, and the coppery smell of blood penetrates the air. Even the smell of grass and manure are thick in the air, from when they've missed and hit the front yard. I think one person even shot the trashcan.

The only thing I can tell is that the sharpshooters are not close, if they're missing. Maybe they just suck.

The sound is deafening, it's an absolute ambush. Someone planned and waited a while to set this up.

I've seen this before, I've done this before. When you have one target in mind, even if you don't have other targets, there's always going to be some collateral damage. In all honesty, the most innocent and sincere one here is Avery, whom is also the target. Luca is still out there.

I'm not a good man anymore, I deserve half of the shit that's happened now and later on in life. Avery, though, she doesn't deserve any of this.

Parts of the house that were ripped apart didn't even have people in them, they were just shredded. I swear they have a group of guys, probably at least ten to fifteen, surrounding the house and just laying some mad fire down. If we take out one guy, another just picks up where he left off.

I feel extremely nauseous as I try to protect my head and everything else from the sharp shards of glass streaming by. The noise is intense, like multiple explosions are happening everywhere: left, right, down and even behind me.

I don't see Avery anymore. Several of the guys that ran in with Mac are on the floor moaning and crying out in pain. Every part of me wants to see how bad they're hurt. I'm not doing shit until I can figure out where the fuck Avery went. She was just ten feet in front of me a few seconds ago.

More of mine and Vito's men have started to run in. I can hear yelling outside the house, so thankfully they figured out what was going on and they're after the sharpshooters themselves.

"Avery!" The panic starts to build up in me. I can feel it, wanting to explode, to do everything it can to get away. I need to find my girl and I need to find her now.

If I let go, I'm not sure which monster I'll turn into.

Mac walks back over to me holding onto his shoulder tight.

"You okay man?" I asked him once I see the blood squeezing through his fingers.

Mac gives me a tight nod and continues looking around. He's searching for more of his men, or ones that might be alive. I know he's also looking for Avery, too.

Screams can be heard outside, in addition to the grunts and moans of pain from inside.

The house has filled with smoke and a metallic smell from the guns, the blood, sweat and tears of those that have been hit.

It's so hard to see anything. I take my time as my foot works around on the floor, trying to find anyone or anything.

Taking a shuddering breath, I realize I might not like what I find. I just pray to God that my girl's okay. Others have been yelling out her name, too, no answer. If this fucking place would just clear out, then we can figure out where the hell Avery's at.

A chill goes through me as I realize we have dead bodies on the floor from people that were shot. By the vicinity of where Avery was. I start to work my way through the darkness faster, as I realize that Avery could likely be one of these people laying on the floor.

I look around at the people standing up, I haven't seen Vito for a while. I know he was elsewhere in the house, this is not good.

I see Mac and carefully make my way over to him. Thankfully he didn't get much farther than when he just talked to me. "Our top priorities right now are Vito and Avery. No one can seem to find either one of them."

The guys use flashlights on their phones, or flashlights that they've been able to find around the house. At least they can make out images on the floor better.

Vito was found in one of the hallways past the foyer over by Garrett and Arya's office. Thankfully he was just knocked out, probably from the blast. Most of us let out the breath we've been holding when Vito walks out with other guards.

"I got knocked on my ass," Vito says as he fights to regain his consciousness.

Within a minute, all of us are searching for Avery. Most have moved on to different areas, but not Mac. Mac starts thoroughly checking the guys that have fallen in the foyer, right around the time it happened. Others have fallen that came running in after.

"Got her," Mac yells as we all start to work our way over there.

Every inch of floor isn't covered in wounded men or dead bodies. They are awkwardly spaced out. Unluckily for them, though, the only thing that matters is Avery. I move fast, I try not to step on anybody but I know I've accidentally kicked a couple of men, but no noise followed. My heart tightens at that fact. This has to be killing Mac. He's like a father figure and an older brother to all these guys.

I bend down next to Mac, my hands won't stop shaking. Right now I only see two guys laying on their stomachs.

I inch my head a little closer and look down. That's when I notice the familiar hand I love so much.

"Avery," I shout as Mac and I painstakingly lift the two dead bodies of our guys off a beaten and bruised Avery, thankfully there's no critical wounds on her.

My girl looks at me in shock, her eyes are wide open. I could tell she's trying to talk but she just can't seem to find the words.

"I got you," I say to her as I lift her up. I glance toward Mac. "Everybody taken care of outside?"

"Yes, boss," Mac says as he starts to make sure we have a good path leading out of the house.

Vito Romano is in shock. It's apparent. You would think the more times you do this, the more you get used to it, but that's not true. His humility is strong to go through this again, to see his granddaughter like that, it's probably taking a major toll on him.

I glanced at Vito and Mac remembering that day. They're doing the same thing, both of them are really deep in thought. We needed this today to help us move on because we lost a lot of people. It will never take away the pain, but hopefully this will ease it.

We offered Avery, Arya and Garrett to come with us but they all refused.

Avery just wants this behind her, and the Stones

haven't had to deal with any of this shit for so long, since they were silent members of the Romano's, and now it's blowing up in their face, so that can't be easy.

I go outside and start to walk around, I'm able to pinpoint a few areas that the sharpshooters were at. Some were close, but most were a few blocks away. Easier escape that way. When our guys started taking out the closer shooters, the other's packed up their shit and left.

I smile when I remember how much the guards have taken to Avery. Not one of them sat and watched when things started to go down. When they saw those red dots on her chest, they all moved into action. They were willing to give their life to save hers, and some of them did.

Avery knows this, as well, and that's why she's having a hard time coming back from everything. Vito's a lot better now, I think he's just more pissed.

When I get into the backyard over by the shed, I hear a strange noise. There shouldn't be anything out here making noise. The shooters that were still here going after us were either killed or they just left.

I look a little closer and open the door to the shed and then I start to laugh. "Well damn, you're going to make everybody's day, aren't you?"

It's the little things that matter. This surprise isn't going to fix everything, but the pain will be lifted.

CHAPTER 2

Avery

After tossing and turning most the night, I finally give in as I roll over on the other side of the bed. The frustration is getting to me from not being able to sleep.

I groan as I wipe the sleep out of my eyes and drag myself out of the very comfortable but extremely lonely bed.

Damn I miss the guys so much. I just wish they would come back, even though they haven't been gone that long. I know they wanted to check on the house to make sure that everything was okay. After everything that happened, I don't want to be away from Asher or my grandfather for even a minute.

I was able to finish school online, far away. There are a couple people that I miss at Blackwood Academy, there are also a couple teachers I miss seeing. The teachers that make you feel safe, not the ones that are scared of everybody and everything and will bow down to one of the richer kids in an instant.

No, I miss the ones that love their job, that do whatever they can to make you feel like you're at home and comfortable.

Getting used to doing school online wasn't hard for me at all. Tate and I had done it for a couple weeks before. I'm not lonely, I still have everybody around me. All of us do our work together, for an hour a day.

Even Tate's grades went up, most likely from us all helping her and I know I did some of the work for her, but we all deserve to graduate, and thankfully we did.

Nothing feels better than being able to get my diploma. I wish I could've had the experience in person, though.

I'm not that upset about graduation. My parents are not here to see me graduate. I think graduation day would be harder if I had to walk across the stage. On a good note, I do have a grandfather now.

I wash my hands quickly and dry them off as I make my way out of the bathroom.

Life throws you unimaginable curve balls all the time. Thinking about it, because of the loss of my parents, I now have Asher and my grandfather, but then again, I miss my parents so much.

I wanted to go to prom, have a normal teenage life, well as normal as I can for being a Romano. And really who's to say I won't run into my grandfather later.

I've already missed sixteen years with my grandfather, I'm glad I've been with him for the last year almost.

I lost something important to me, but from that loss I gained a lot, too. The world I live in is fucking crazy and things change instantly, sometimes way too fast. For now, I'm holding onto everything important. I refuse to lose anything else.

We have been in New York for six months now, ever since the Stone's house turned into target practice.

We're just sitting here, waiting. Luca is out there somewhere, we just don't know where. And for some reason both my grandfather and Asher think he's living right next door to the Mancini compound.

If I go out too far, for sure I'll end up dead. Well, they told all of us that.

I know that the guys are just being careful. For God's sake, Vito Romano and Asher Mancini decided that we were going across the country. They failed to mention it or ask any of us. Just packed us all up and told us to leave.

The one I thought would hate this the most would definitely be Tate. But, ironically she was the most excited to get away from all the drama. I also believe that she was happy to go back home and not have to worry about being killed or beat to shit by her brothers.

I would have to say that I'm the one that's most bummed out. Not just about graduating since I had to leave. I'm always on guard, yeah, I know that comes with the lifestyle. But I am always on guard more so than other people are. It seems like so many want to hurt and kill me.

Before my life was easy, not easy but more normal and less stressful.

I knew something was going down when Asher and my gramps disappeared into closed meetings for a while. I figured we had to leave but I expected we'd go back to Chicago. I know Chicago, I miss Chicago. I barely knew New York at all. From what I understand, the Romano's don't even do that much business here. My grandfather likes it that way and chooses not to go after the whole East Coast.

I am extremely grateful for this decision. But, I'm fucked either way. The man I love runs it, or my grandfather runs it. There will always be shit I have to deal with. Death will always be around me. And life will be so little, so short and unexpected.

Don't get me wrong, we had to leave California. I refuse to throw a tantrum like a toddler, over and over again, except for in my head. California was out for good now, unless Luca dies, and after talking to my grandfather I learned that Chicago is, too.

Even though I'm almost positive it was Luca, we still need to be careful. We're not one-hundred percent sure who ordered the attack on us.

Deep down we all know it was Luca. Chicago would be one of the first places he'd go to look for me, at the Romano compound. It's the smartest thing to do and that's what I would do. Go to where everything started.

My parent's house is long gone, which is a good thing because it doesn't even look the same after the fire. It's a total tear down. My grandfather still owns the land. I don't know what he plans to do with it but I'm hoping that he'll put in like a sweet little park for the kids or something with a happy memory, not a memorial.

We've been at the Mancini estate for six months now, six very long months. And in that time I have still not been able to see this whole place.

I remember the day we got here we were also shaken and upset. Nobody wanted to go through this again, *nobody wanted to do this again*. This is the new normal for us, I guess.

I can tell myself that twenty times and I'll never get used to it.

When we came up on the house, it felt like we were going into an old plantation estate. But I've never seen a house this big before. I've had my share of being in big houses, because my family and we're definitely not poor, but nothing can compare to the monstrosity that is this house.

I figured it to be cold and lonely, no, it's very warm and welcoming. There's wood everywhere accented by natural paints; brown, green and yellow. It makes it feel so cozy. Asher's a freaking clean freak, especially the floor. Something to do with his childhood.

My favorite room is the library. The whole thing is painted black. I never thought it would work in a library, but it does, it makes it more masculine. A perfect fit for the Mancini's. I fell in love instantly, there's eight freaking full size sofas in here. They're mostly rugged leather that looks like it's been beaten to shit. I bet they bought this brand-new for fifteen-grand, yeah, that kind of furniture.

Now, if I can shorten the size of this damn castle, it would be perfect. Asher and Tate were telling me that there's almost thirty-thousand square-feet in here with eight bedrooms and twelve bathrooms.

I find it funny how they say only eight bedrooms because I've been walking around and viewing part of the house, when I'm not locking myself in the library. There are multiple spare bedrooms; changing rooms, wrapping rooms, playrooms, there's even a movie theater room, but we haven't used that one yet. Not sure why, we all love the movies.

I was shocked when my grandpa decided to stay with us. I know that had to be hard for him, because this isn't his domain, this isn't his area, and these are not his people. Even though he probably brought around seventy-five guys with him. Luckily the property has houses and shops all over it. I don't know exactly what's here, there are over seven-hundred freaking acres.

Between the Romano men and the Mancini men, we've been held up here and safe. That's all that matters until we decide to make our next move. I have no clue what that'll be, maybe one day they'll tell us.

I was shocked that the guys decided to wait this long but they wanted things to cool down before we figure out what we're going to do.

Tate is looking at colleges, I know she wants to go. Which is a shocker because my friend at school is not a go-getter. I believe she just wants a life out of the one that we have, and I don't blame her. Did I mention that there were three pools, three? *Three damn pools*. Who in the hell needs three pools?

Everybody's located in different wings of the house on different floors. Sometimes, it takes for freaking ever to find someone.

Asher was working a bit when we first got back, so Tate decided to give me an awesome tour.

Now if we could only split this house into fourths, then I would be happy.

It's just an aberration really. I don't even understand how people can find their children unless they have tracking software in here.

It's weird going to bed at night with Asher in the master bedroom. I've seen houses smaller than the master bedroom.

I go back to my favorite leather couch in the library and curl up. I like to read but I'm not obsessed with it, I just like the comfort, the simplicity of being in here.

"There you are," Tate says as she skips toward me.

"Fuck, you scared the shit out of me." Tate is very quiet when she moves around, but she has a fiery storm that follows her everywhere. Calm in the beginning followed by whatever she decides to rain down on you.

"Sorry." She is sorry, but she thinks it's funny. "Have you heard anything?" I shake my head no. We've both been waiting for news. The kind that will dictate our lives and what the future will hold for us. College for Tate, but for me, I have no freaking clue.

"Bummer," Tate mumbles to herself. She looks back up at me and plasters her face with a beautiful, welcoming smile. Not fake, very real. "Okay, I've got Marcus coming to do my nails." She gives me a wink and then skips right back out of the library.

Marcus is one of the local guys that is a master at nails. I wouldn't know, I tried it once and have never done it again.

Since we're not allowed to leave, I imagine she paid out the ass to get him to come here, we're not exactly close to town, either.

Every single person we know or have been hanging around with, has gone with us to New York. I'm not talking about Paisley and her bitch crew, only our people, the one's we're close to.

Arya and Garrett stayed for a week or two, but then they went off to London. I'll be honest, I do miss them a lot, but I know how happy they are right now. Most of their business trips take them to London, anyway, so why not just move there? The only reason they kept coming back was for me.

I love the Stones so much. They went out of their way to make sure I was okay and had a safe place to go after the hell I went through.

We still talk like once every couple weeks. It's like it was before, Arya still makes sure I'm eating and doing everything I'm supposed to do. It's different with Garrett, because he would ask questions about the house or tell me what to do. Now he just has nothing to say, it's kind of awkward but it's more awkward for him, because he feels uncomfortable, but he tries.

Sadness fills my eyes, even though we're not exactly sure who attacked the Stone's house, we know. We know that it was Luca, we know that his sick and twisted mind made them come after us, come after me, I know that Luca is not doing this because he loves me, or he wants me to be the mother of his children. No, Luca is doing this because it's all a game to him.

I imagine this is his finest and deadliest game that he's ever played, to date.

It's a challenge for him since he wasn't able to kill me when he killed my parents. He was unable to get to me when he destroyed the Stone's house. And he was unable to get to me when he got into the Stone's house, killing several guys, and pissing off Mac, one of the few people I respect.

Mac, that guy hasn't been able to relax since that

day. He's a father and older brother figure to all of his guys. I love him just as much as they do.

Luca is more deadly now since I have his attention. He will do whatever it takes to win. More lives will be lost, innocent and undeserving. Those are the ones that matter to me. I never wanted to be in a position where somebody else can die because of me. Even though it's not directly my fault, I'll have to live with this for the rest of my life.

I've had this talk with Asher and Tate so many times they tell me I need to get out of my head and get on with my life. The world that we live in today, all of this is the normal everyday occurrence. Hold on to the ones you love and don't take anything for granted.

That night when I was heading back up to Asher, all the images fled back into my head. Maybe because I'm thinking about Luca right now, who knows.

I couldn't realize why Mac, several of the guards and Asher were freaking out when they looked at me. And I didn't find out until one of them straight up tackled me like a football player.

The laser lights were invisible at first but after Mac tackled me and then Asher jumped on me, I could see them everywhere. On the walls, on the floor, on the ceiling, coming in through the glass. It seemed like every inch was overtaken by them. They must've had hundreds of guys outside.

I start to chuckle to myself and whisper. "That's funny." The HOA is just as sick as Luca.

At least one-hundred guys attacked us, I'm not exactly sure. Vito and Asher don't tell me anything, so that's a guesstimate. The outside of the house is blown to shit. Chunks of concrete have fallen, glass is shattered everywhere. The lawn looks like a bomb went off.

We expected to have problems with the HOA demanding everything to be fixed up. What we didn't expect was only one complaint and that was for the windows. Not the hole in the roof, or the chunks of the house lying on the ground. No, windows were the only problem. They got them fixed and left everything else alone.

Vito hasn't talked that much about it, but I'm fairly certain the Stones will never move back to that house. They couldn't get away fast enough after it happened. I never told anyone, but they begged me to go with them. My eyes water at that thought. I miss them so much, just having that closeness with family, and Arya has been like a mom to me.

My head snaps over to the door and I yank the blanket off my lap. I can hear screaming coming from the foyer. Not the kind of murder, death, Luca is here, the happy kind. One that is promising very good news.

Now I'm up and jogging to the front of the house where I heard the noise coming from. Thankfully the library is close. If it was on the other side, I would've never known anybody entered.

As soon as I reach the foyer I start screaming and

the tears freshly flow down my face. I run awkwardly past my grandfather, Asher and all the other guys. I drop to my knees, carefully trying not to hurt him. I wrap my arms around a very pissed off Sneaker.

Tate is sitting on the floor next to me crying. Even though this little shit is a total ass, he's family. Damn, did we miss him. No one could find him, we even had people looking all the time. Arya is heartbroken. I look up at Asher with tears in my eyes as I stand up, cradling a usually grouchy asshole, but he seems very content right now. He missed us, too.

I kiss Asher and then give my grandfather a quick hug.

"In the shed in the back." I have no idea how that little shit survived but he did, he definitely deserves to be a Mancini and Romano.

Tate and I take a selfie with Sneaker as we send it off to Arya. It won't be long till we hear her screaming. Even though they're a world away, Sneaker is their baby just as much as he was ours.

He might only be a cat that I didn't get along with very much, but he's also a symbol of hope, I feel that we're all going to be all right. *Welcome home.*

CHAPTER 3

LUCA

I chuckle to myself as I glance out the window leading to the long main road to the Mancini estate. If those fuckers only knew that I was a couple miles down the road, they would shit themselves.

I wanted to be as close to Avery as I could. I feel more grounded when I'm closer to her.

We got lucky. We found an abandoned house with only a caretaker that comes every so often, and thankfully for us it wasn't shit. The house was actually kept up. I hate when I have to live beneath my means.

Of course we got lucky but the caretaker didn't. He was an older man. He reminded me a lot of my grandfather for a second there. I thought we could just let him go with no problems. But I knew that bitch would sing like a canary. I had a couple of my guys just take him out in the backyard and end him. They were out there for a while, I wonder if they had him dig his own grave.

I laugh, that man did not look like the grave digging type, maybe that's why they've been out there for so long.

I know that Avery and the rest of them have been in hiding in the Mancini house, thinking they're safe for the past six months. I wanted to relocate here right away and find a place, but I'm grateful that we waited for at least four months. The longer you stay in a place, it's harder to disguise yourself. And seeing how I've been on the run for the past year, I understand.

I can hear Avery's voice echo through the computer screen as her and Tate start to laugh. I laugh, too, but not in a funny way. I'm mocking her. She should be with me. I shouldn't even be in this dreadful state. I'd rather head back to Chicago, back home.

Now I am stuck right here in the middle of nowhere New York. At least I can see were a couple of the rich people live. The Mancini's like their privacy. Most people wouldn't want to live too close to the mafia, look what happened to this insufferable fool. Guy's only been taking care of the house.

When we first came up here I thought a huge problem we would face is how to find out information on the inside. How do we find out what they're planning? How do we find out if they know that we're down the street?

I laugh. "Stupid Mancini's." I have two guys that are

working for me inside the house. I almost had a third but he was a fucking pussy, too afraid of Asher and Vito Romano to worry about getting revenge. That's all this is for the guys that are helping me get much deserved revenge.

Cameras are installed in every single room, hallway, kitchen, garage, backyard, everywhere. The only place that I can't get them in, is in the bathrooms. That's what they told me, anyway. That's fine by me, I really don't want to watch somebody shit.

I wouldn't mind watching Avery or even Tate taking a shower, together. My dick swells. Bastard always gets hard and ready whenever I think about Avery and everything she promised me and still has yet to give.

The master bedroom is the one I wanted more than anything, but Asher has a security code on it. Fucker has a retina scanner. My guys don't have access to that yet. So him and Avery are the only ones that are able to go in there. My men have a plan, so hopefully we'll be in there sooner than later.

I'm hoping to see my girl have some alone time with herself, touching herself, thinking about me. It's better the cameras aren't installed, because if I see him touch her I'll probably lose my shit.

"Fuck!" I scream as the thought of him laying one finger on her enters my mind in full detail, nothing is left out.

The door slams open as my right hand guy Seth

eases his head around the door, weary. "You okay, boss?" I give him a quick nod making sure he knows to back the fuck up, before I lose my shit even more. He listens and quickly closes the door.

I sit back down getting myself together. To see him close to Avery makes my blood boil, the all-consuming rage grips and sucks the life right out of me. I know I possess quite the temper. I find it ironic that Avery had such a problem being with me, but she's just with the same kind of animal I am, *a boss.*

A thought goes through my head. *What if Avery has no choice?* What if she has wanted to be with me all this time, but she's not able to. Yeah, the parents dying in a fiery blaze will be a problem for us down the road. She'll come to understand why it had to be done, maybe she already does. Maybe the Mancini's are in her head, feeding her lies. Things that aren't true, things about me that I could never do to her.

I cringe deep down. I know that's not true. I haven't fully lost my head but there's always a possibility. It makes my heart constrict when I think that she could be there reaching out for me. I look at the computer screen and see her and Tate playing with an ugly ass cat.

I hear static from another monitor, informing me of another conversation taking place. As much as I don't want to, I look away from Avery and focus on Asher's office.

I have men assigned to watch the monitors twenty-four seven, but most of the time I find myself in front. I just can't get enough of watching her, if I can't be with her, at least I could see her every day.

Asher and Mac are going over details as they did before. I already know about their plans and their deliveries for the day. I get up and head out toward the kitchen, ignoring my men as they give me tight smiles. It's better this way, small talk is never needed, there's nothing to talk about, so why bother.

We found out so much information from having the cameras and audio equipment in the house. They are the size of a pea, but flat. They're very easy to hide. I'm surprised Asher and his team haven't done a thorough check. They probably figured they didn't need to because they were safe in their compound.

I've been collecting information. I know at least sixty percent of the Mancini's business dealings. Sixty fucking percent just by listening in on these audio devices. I know I should probably have them pulled out because they're going to start noticing, especially when we start taking over their shipments. I can't allow myself to do it yet, though. I like seeing Avery, and honestly if I'm caught, who gives a shit?

The info I have now is gold. A few times a year the Mancini's run very big shipments. It all makes sense, this lowers the risk of them getting caught, less time to deal with the police. A huge shipment every three months destroys the demand of tiny runs once a week, or once every other week.

The big one is coming from Russia by barge.

Asher and Vito have guys stationed in southern and eastern Maine. The barge can slip in without having to go through border protection. Payoffs and a deserted location will make this work wonderfully. Soon, when I take down the Mancini's and Romano's, I will continue to keep doing things this way.

It's like learning all the inside information without having to pay for it. That makes my life ten times easier.

I grab a few bottles of water in the fridge and head back to the office staring straight ahead and not making eye contact with anybody. If I had time to talk I would come and sit out here or we'd go to the fucking park.

We could've made our move for Avery a while ago. We have extensive knowledge with the blueprints that were provided to me on where the fuck everything is in the house. She would've never seen it coming.

She could've been with me for the past couple months. She would've been my queen. While she still will be, just a bit longer. I want heirs like crazy. That's Avery's job; fucking and popping out babies.

I growl remembering how my father, the head of the Delano family, wanted to knock off all the Romano's. If I didn't listen to him, I know without a doubt Avery and I would still be together, she loves me, well she did once.

It's time to figure out a plan and just go in there and

get her. There are too many men to do the whole guns blazing. There are other ways I just need to find one that'll work, hopefully within the next few days. They've all been cooped up in that house for a while, that's not going to last much longer.

I have a feeling very soon that they're going to change residences and I'll have to start all over.

"Fuck," I growl to myself. "Seth!" I scream toward the doors. Seth being a good soldier, he opens it right away.

"Get everybody in here, it's time." It's time for me to get my girl.

CHAPTER 4

AVERY

I gasp for air, as I strain to open my eyelids. When I finally do I can see a very happy looking Asher smirking at me. The covers are on the other side of the bed and he's right between my legs. What must've woke me up is the fact that he's slowly removing my clothes.

I smile and sit up a little faster than I normally should. I'm a little too excited for this right now, which he notices and it makes him laugh. Oh well, I don't fucking care, I'm horny as hell.

Normally I'm not this way, I'm usually shy and likely to avoid people at all costs. This morning, though, there's some kind of spark, something igniting within my body, setting every cell alive.

I gently push Asher on his back. At first his eyes are a little wide wondering what the fuck I'm doing, but then he gets it and he smiles. The bastard is laying down with his hands under his head. Thankfully he's naked and I don't have to yank anything off. His leg is slightly bent. Ready and waiting to see what I'm gonna do to him. If he only knew.

I take my sweet time as I straddle my glorious god. I ease down ever so slowly. We both suck in a needed breath of air when I start to move down, excruciatingly slow, inch by inch. It won't be long before one of us snaps and I'm going to make sure it's not me. I smile at him, he knows exactly what I'm thinking.

I was able to do this for several seconds before Asher grabs my hip and yanks me down to the hilt. Plunging into me. I groan and shiver. Asher has lost his smirk.

"Move," he commands as he starts to gyrate his hips. I love that he's letting me run the show right now, and he's not taking over. It would only take seconds for him to change the whole situation.

I move back and forth for a few minutes before I start to elevate myself and bounce. Reliving every blissful second as it happens. He's yanking down on my hips several times. I know he wants me to go faster but this feels so good and I love the pace that I've got right now.

Apparently Asher doesn't like that. He quickly sits himself up grabbing me and holding us chest to chest. There's not that much room to move but there's enough. Asher moves us over to the edge of the bed and stands up, taking me with him. I'm holding on for dear life but I don't even care. Everything feels euphoric, blissful. I don't want to move even for a second away from this gorgeous man.

At least he lasted longer this time. In the beginning he would never let me be on top. He's a man that likes to be in control of everything, even our fucking.

I groan when he pulls out, flipping me on my stomach, yanking me down to the edge of the bed. Before I even have a chance to turn my head, Asher is straddling me from behind.

It doesn't take long before my body starts to shake. I bite the sheet that my face is pushed into and groan. My hands are positioned next to the sides of my head, gripping the sheet. After we finish, we'll need to buy new bedding. I'm ripping it to shreds with my fingernails and my teeth.

"Now baby," Asher whispers in my ear. His hands are pressed tightly on my hips, almost like he's touching the bone. He makes sure to keep us joined together as he relentlessly pounds into me.

"Asher!" I scream out as he pumps several more times and releases into me on a growl. I chuckle lightly to myself as I scream his name and he grunts. It shows how different we are.

Asher quickly makes his way to the bathroom to clean himself off and bring me back a rag. A week after we started having sex, he made an appointment for me to go to the doctor and get on birth control. He told me, "we don't need any little Mancini's right now. When I'm fucking you, I'll be bare."

Asher checks his phone while he puts on his jeans. I'm thinking about getting dressed with him but I'm not sure if I want to get out of bed.

"Get ahold of the other guys, we have a meeting, only the top people." Asher hangs up before he gets a response. I'm sure he was talking to Mac. Mac has been with the Romano's forever. He's been helping some until Doppler gets back later today. I'm not sure what's going on with Doppler, but it's not good for him to be away from Asher and the Mancini's for so long. Maybe I should ask. I've always been curious, but I also figure that people's business is their own business. If he wanted everybody to know, we all would've known.

Asher heads into the bathroom to brush his teeth most likely and finish getting ready for the meeting. I jump out of bed, I'm still naked with barely enough damn time for me to get dressed.

Thankfully I locate my cellphone on my freaking nightstand, usually I fall asleep with the fucker in the bed and it can take me anywhere from five to twenty-five minutes to find the damn thing every day.

I quickly call Tate. "Avery?" Tate groans in the phone as she answers. "Have you looked at the fucking time, it's only eight AM, psycho woman."

I'm laughing so hard at her that the tears are pouring out of my eyes. I'm not usually a morning person, none of us have been lately because there's not that much to do except for sleep.

"A meeting has been called." I don't say anything else, she'll get it.

"When?" Tate snaps, I can hear rustling as she must be up running around getting ready. That makes me also get my ass into gear as I throw on a pair of leggings and a tight tank top. It is summer and we're in New York. Plus, it's comfortable as fuck.

The phone is still on for both of us, but neither one of us talks since we know the other's getting ready. Now this is awkward. I would like to finish without being on the phone.

"I'll meet you down there in five," I say into the phone. I'm not sure if Tate is brushing her teeth or what she's doing but she just gives me a muffled okay.

I hang up and get to work, brushing my hair and throwing it into a ponytail. I would love to take a shower, because as soon as I walk down there I feel like everybody will know what we did. I wonder if Asher took a shower.

I go as slow I can, quietly making my way down to the foyer. I glance around for Tate in a full circle before I spot her hiding off in an enclave behind the stairs, she quickly waves me over.

Both of us without making any noise watch some of the guys go by. Vito and one of his guards has already walked into Asher's office.

Tate nudges me with her elbow. "The bathroom's

right there." She points as she whispers. "That connects to Asher's office. If we find the right spot we should be able to hear everything." Tate smiles wickedly and I look a little nervous. Shit, has my girl been listening in on these meetings?

Both of us put our heads down as we quietly make our way toward the bathroom. Tate puts her arm through mine. We're almost there when the front door slams open.

A very bloody, bruised and very pissed Carter stomps and grunts his way right by us. He glares at Tate, giving her a look of hate. What happened between those two?

"Did he do something to you?" I whisper in Tate's ear. I've only received that look from one person in my life, and it was Luca.

The look he gave her is one of pure hate, and that makes me very nervous.

"No, nothing like that." Tate says as she quickly works her way toward the bathroom, leaving me behind and letting me know that our conversation is definitely over. It makes me more nervous because Tate and I are totally open with each other about everything. If we have a chance, I'll tell her about this morning. We're just that good of friends, but she might not enjoy listening about her uncle that way. This new revelation is leaving my stomach sour and very concerned. This man is emanating anger. This is definitely not a good feeling in my stomach right now. Tate and I need to really talk about this. Carter seems like a psychopath.

"Luckily for us," Tate whispers as we enter the bathroom, "this one is rarely used, that's because people don't even know it's back here. The little walkway in here is so dark there's not even a light out there. Which makes it perfect. Asher almost fixed it, but decided against it. That's only because I begged him. I told Asher that it's great for hiding spots and it makes me feel safe if anybody ever enters the house."

That does make sense, I think as I nod to her. I like the fact that we have this little area and nobody knows where we're at. In actuality it does make me feel safer.

We have to move between the toilet and the fancy bathtub that's the weakest point on the wall. That's the place where Tate pinpricked a couple areas through the drywall, making it easier to eavesdrop. After she shows me this, I just laugh at my psychotic friend. "That's freaking awesome," I tell her as I continue to quietly chuckle.

From what we can understand the guys are still just getting their shit together. I wrap my arm around Tate and give her a tight squeeze. "Maybe we'll finally get to leave this place." She nods at me frantically.

We make sure that we're as quiet as we possibly can be. If someone in that other room leans against the wall and hears us whisper, it's all over.

We'll never find out what they're saying anymore.

Tate and I have both demanded that we have a right to be in these meetings but we're not high up. Whatever the hell that means. We don't give a shit about the ins and outs of the business. We just want to listen in and being part of shit that concerns us right now, like leaving.

As the guys start to talk about stupid stuff, neither one of us pay attention to drop-off locations, shipments and their plans for getting whatever at these locations. I'm a hundred percent sure everything is illegal, probably guns and drugs. I just hope they don't mention women or children because that would just end it for me.

I've been able to hear when every guy speaks. Tate and I are able to pick out who's here and who's not. As soon as Doppler speaks I squeeze her hand and mouth, 'Doppler' and she nods. He must be back.

So far we know that Asher and Vito are in the meeting. There is also Mac, Carter, Walker, Liam, and Noah who all lock themselves in. Not wanting to let anybody else in there or listen to what they have to say. They even have a couple guards stationed outside the door, keeping those out that are not welcome.

"Shit," Tate says as she starts squeezing her legs together. "I have to pee so bad." I start to chuckle and quickly slap my hand over my mouth, I don't want to get caught. Tate is annoyed as hell, she's always loved listening in on these meetings. She quickly walks away hoping to sneak out and use another bathroom, without getting caught. Someone peeing in here would definitely give us away.

In the time that she's gone she hasn't missed anything, they just keep talking about the same old shit, deliveries and drop-offs. Stuff that bores the fuck out of us.

"Whatever Asher says is final." My grandfather's stern voice rings out through the room. "This man has not lost one shipment or gotten one guy in trouble in years. That's almost unheard of." I can hear my grandfather patting Asher on the back. I don't know if it's possible but I swear my heart gets a little bigger.

Tate shuffles back into the room a little loudly, and I wave my hand telling her to shut the fuck up.

At that point I notice something is going on with my friend, who's holding her stomach looking like she hasn't even been to the bathroom and she's white as a ghost, making her already pale skin look sickly. I lift both of my hands up in a 'what' motion.

Tate takes out her phone and hands it to me. Right as I start to look at the picture I can hear Asher's voice boom through the tiny little holes in the bathroom.

"We have a mole." The whole room goes silent, even my grandfather doesn't say anything. Dammit! I wish I could see everybody's expressions.

I look up at Tate to see if she's shocked but she's still staring at the phone that's in my hand.

I look down at it. I can't really make out the image. It's a man standing around the corner but close enough to be able to hear through the main office doors. It looks like he's even close with some of the guards. In one of the other pictures Tate shows me, he's writing in his notebook at a different angle.

"I think you found the mole." Tate nods frantically looking at the wall we had been listening to and back to the phone. "You have to tell them it's Rocco." She sighs in defeat as a lone tear slowly escapes from her eye. We both know that she has to let them know because this could hurt us later. The thing that sucks is we will never be able to come back here and listen again.

Now we both feel defeated, but it's the right thing to do.

Tate sends the pictures to Asher and we just wait. He didn't stop right away and look at his phone when he was talking. Giving ideas on the mole and how they can rectify the situation.

Tate and I just sit there quietly, her eyes are glossed over from the tears. I know my friend is hurting, not just because she's gonna lose her hiding place, she's gonna lose her brother. Everyone in this life knows how it works. One day she was hoping for a normal relationship with them, but it's never going to happen. My heart breaks for her.

Even though I don't have my parents anymore, Tate once told me. "Sometimes you just need to make and create your own family." I want her to know that I'm her family, all of us are. I don't think Carter would fall in this category, but the other guys do.

Voices are hushed and I can make out whispering tones. "They saw it," Tate mumbles.

And that they did. We can hear Rocco scream as they open the office door and yank him violently inside. The bathroom door is opened slowly as Carter makes his way inside, never taking his eyes off Tate. The moment she saw him, her head went straight down and she hasn't looked anywhere else.

I need to know what the fuck is going on between these two, but now's not the time. I stand up and move in between them letting them know whatever shit's going down can happen later, not now.

He gives me a look that I can't even describe, one of hate and annoyance. It doesn't last long because Asher pushes his way in and grabs my hand. At the same time Carter grabs Tate and we're being dragged back to the master bedroom.

Tate is violently shoved into the room, landing on her side. He looks down at Tate who happens to be staring up at him. Her eyes are no longer glossy, she's hysterically crying.

"Thank you," Asher says with sadness in his eyes. This was the only way we can get information in this house, because nobody likes to share.

Asher gives me a kiss on the mouth and then looks at both of us. "Stay put. There will be guards to make sure you guys do."

When Asher leaves, I can hear a click from the outside. I move closer to examine the door because I don't ever remember there being a lock on the outside, one I've never seen anyway. Probably just had maintenance install it five minutes ago, to lock us in here.

Mac comes in the room a minute later just to hang out with us. We're thankful, he's our favorite out of all of them except for Doppler.

"The mole fucked up Asher's perfect record." Tate and I look at him and then each other. "Luca's men knew about the drop that Carter was supervising, and he barely made it out. Just avoid him today if you can." When Mac says the last part he looks at Tate.

Maybe that's why he is so mad and looks horrible. Maybe he thought Tate was the mole and everything was her fault. I don't know, I'd like to be able to figure this out, but she's not telling me everything. It's like she's terrified.

"That's not good. Is Carter going to be okay?" Mac nods his head. Tate doesn't say anything, she just stares at the floor in her own little world. I can't even tell what she's thinking or how she's feeling, especially since I don't know everything that's going on with her right now.

Mac gives us both a comforting hug and heads back to the office. I have a feeling that Asher or my grandfather sent Mac here to make us feel better. I'm grateful for that.

I sit down next to Tate on the floor. "At least that

explains a lot of what's wrong with Carter. He looks like they beat the shit out of him." Tate just sniffles letting me know she's not gonna let anything go.

Dammit! My friend should be able to tell me everything. What is going on with those two? I'm determined to find out.

I don't get a good feeling from Carter, and why he's so deplorable to Tate all the time.

A thought hits me at that time. "Does he have something on you? Or did you do something? Or do you have a horrible secret he knows?"

Tate gives me a soft smile and squeezes my hand and then shakes her head no to everything. I knew right then, I needed to leave it alone for at least today.

I wrap my arm around her, even though they got the mole that's one brother that she's probably never going to see again. Both of us heard his screams as they were pulling him into the room. Even after everything he's done to her, she still worries about him. She would probably even worry about Armani if he was still here, too.

I grab Tate by the hand and pull her up to the bed. I get her settled in comfortably and then I wrap myself around her. "It's gonna be okay, Vito and Asher will handle everything. Just go to sleep."

She nods letting me know that she's listening. I snuggle as close as I can get to her. It doesn't take long before we're both out cold.

CHAPTER 5

ASHER

I drop down into my office chair and lean my head back. My hands rubbing over my face and running through my hair. I can't believe those two were listening the whole time.

I start to laugh. Tate explained why she didn't want anything done with this area over here, any lights added or anything else. This was her eavesdropping zone. I laugh a little more causing everybody to look at me. It's not like she'll find another place to go.

Even Vito, Mac and Doppler are chuckling a little at both the girls, even though I am a little shocked to find Avery there. I expect this from Tate, she's our wild child. Not Avery, she's a good girl.

A heavy weight has been lifted off my shoulders, but my heart feels constricted. For the longest time Vito and I couldn't figure out how others were able to pin point our drop-off and pickup locations. Everything we had going on. Even some of our private meetings were disturbed.

Luckily for all of us, I'm still careful with everything. I always send a shit ton of my guys to meetings, to everything we have going on. Can't take a fucking chance in this world.

God, fucking Rocco. I can't believe he did this. His normal smirk is wiped off his face and replaced with fear. He knows what can happen and he knows there's nothing I can do about it, I won't do anything about it.

He put all of us in a dangerous situation, including himself. I am positive that he's working for Luca. He's family, I'm certain once Luca didn't need him anymore, he'd get rid of him.

I shake my head, even Vito, Mac and the others are quite disturbed by this. Yeah, him and his brother are fuck ups but they're still Mancini's. They grew up with the notion our elders passed on to us. 'There is nothing greater than family, protect the name at all costs.' Which they didn't do.

If his parents were here to see him now, they would be disgusted.

I growl out again at the same time that Vito and Mac look in my direction. They must be thinking the same thing. There's no way in hell that Rocco did this himself. And everybody knows that Armani has played his hand in this.

Gino asked if he could leave after everything went

down. We normally don't let people out of the family, they'll be on silent mode, that we can call up any time we ever need them.

Vito did this with the Stones, he was telling me. The Stones have been enjoying their life and haven't had to associate or deal with the family in over ten years, until they got the call for Avery.

Arya is a loving woman, of course she said okay right away, so that's why Vito shipped Avery to California away from her home and away from Luca. At least she was able to stay around family.

The message when it first came in from Tate irritated me. Everybody else knows not to disturb me unless it's important. I knew that it wasn't from any of my guys or they would've just said something. It took almost two minutes until I could check the message.

As soon as I saw the text message, I motioned Mac, Vito, and Carter over to look at it. All of them sprang into action immediately.

Carter ripped open the door and yanked a very shocked and surprised Rocco inside.

The guards grabbed their guns not realizing what the fuck was going on. When they saw who it was they put their guns back and helped assist Carter with dragging a very shit scared looking Rocco into the office.

I currently stare at my nephew sitting in the middle of the office in a single chair, as everyone stands around him in a circle.

Vito's head looks like it's going to explode. I've never seen an Italian so red.

I bet he's wishing that he would've been released just like his brother, Gino. At least Gino has a chance in this world. The boy is studying to be a fucking doctor for God's sake. That shocked us all.

And since he's fully released, we can't call him up like we were able to do with the Stones.

I glance in Mac's direction. "We need to call everybody in. Station some of the men here and then get a few teams ready to go grab Armani. There's no fucking way Rocco pulled this off himself." I stare at Rocco the whole time I talk, making sure that my voice was loud enough for everyone and for him to hear.

His expression confirmed that his brother is involved. More than likely it was Armani's idea.

I get out of my chair fast. My body shoots forward before I even realize what's going on. I don't even feel the hardwood floors beneath me, it's like I'm floating toward Rocco, not even in control of my actions., "You fucking idiot. You know what has to happen now. Should've left like Gino and Armani."

Rocco gasps for air, then starts to suck in as much as he can get into his lungs. Maybe he thought he would just always be okay with Armani. Now he realizes how much he fucked up. In this life you don't fuck up like that and live to tell about it. If my enemies found out that I let him go, everybody would come after me. The fucker doesn't deserve to live even though he's my nephew. What will he do next time when Armani gets into his ear?

I look around the room, Mac and Vito are leaning against the wall both with their arms crossed holding stern expressions. Most of the other guys in the room are just shocked. They know that Armani and Rocco are fuck ups, but they still can't believe the traitorous ways they went after their own family. Neither can I.

"Explain everything, and I'll make sure this ends fast for you," I say to him with my voice slow and calm.

Rocco starts to shake his head back and forth. "No, no, no, don't do me like this, man. We're fucking family."

I go to respond, but out of the corner of my eye I spot Vito stepping forward looking more enraged than I am. Avery is really all he is left, she's the closest to take over the family name.

Without missing a beat and faster than I've seen anybody do it, Vito Romano whips out his gun and shoots Rocco straight in the kneecap.

He slowly walks forward listening to the screams and cries of pain. Drool slides down the side of Rocco's mouth as tears pour down his cheeks, dropping off his chin.

"I don't have time for this. If you don't tell the man what he wants to know, I will start taking you apart piece by piece," Vito says as he takes a step back and folds his arms, his gun still in his hand.

Rocco sobs louder, letting a constant trickle of

liquid fall beneath his seat chair showing that Vito Romano has scared the piss out of my nephew.

A couple of the guards laugh, but quickly press their lips together. Rocco starts to sing like a fucking canary.

WE LISTEN HAPPILY AS ROCCO GOES ON AND ON AND ON for a good hour. He told us everything, even shit we didn't know. Mac started taking notes just so we wouldn't miss anything. I bet it makes him feel better to get it off his chest, even though he was in severe pain. Well that and Vito scared the shit out of him. Torture is not a fun thing for anyone.

Luca had apparently got a hold of Armani and Rocco. I guess he wanted Gino, too, but he was already in school and he refused to have anything to do with the both of them. Smart boy, that's why he's going to stay alive.

Armani was on the deal in no time flat. Which still shows how much he hates and dislikes the rest of us. The little fucker thinks he should be in charge. He would be next in line if I were to die right now obviously, but if I had a child of my own they would be my heir, especially if it was a boy.

Luca had him keep track of everything. Anything he found out, even if it was mundane. He wanted to know everything about Avery; how she was doing, her mood, her clothing, anything he could find out about. That included every single person in this house.

Armani was here occasionally, but not that much. It sounded like he was doing jobs for Luca all the time. Leaving Rocco to take care of everything else. It makes sense now, while we didn't see Armani that much, maybe once or twice a week and Rocco seemed to be here all the time.

Armani's job is to make sure that our people stay straight. If there's anything wrong with shipments or deliveries he takes care of that. Rocco helps him whenever he needs it.

I'm a little bit disappointed in myself. I should've noticed this shit before it escalated so far. Armani and Rocco have been trained their entire lives for their current Mancini jobs. I figured Vito and I got through to them with the beating that they both had, but I guess not.

"When Armani was here, he did help me install surveillance." I stand straight up and all the other guys stiffen, especially Vito.

"Fuck," I mumble out.

"Apparently I wasn't able to get very good notes of everybody and their reactions to anything, I wasn't able to get enough info on Avery. That's when Luca put a knife to my throat and told me that surveillance is going in. He didn't care how I did it as long as it got done."

All of us groan, surveillance is a bitch to get rid of.

To spend the time to make sure it's all gone. Who knows everything they might've heard. Well obviously everything for the past several months since they've had it installed.

Rocco continues. "I was unable to install them in the bathrooms or the master bedroom. The bathrooms nobody ever talks shit in there, and nobody really wants to hear what they're doing. The master bedroom because it's always protected by guards and it's impossible to break into with the eye scanner."

I smile and thank my lucky stars. I wasn't really sure if I wanted to put in a security system to get into my bedroom, but I'm glad I did. It was just a nagging feeling I had, I trust all my men. It shocked the shit out of me when we heard we had a mole.

Mac and Carter grab a very seriously injured Rocco. They drag him around throughout the whole mansion to find the unwanted surveillance.

I would like to leave a message for Luca before everything is removed, but not at this time. "Fuck," I say as I sigh. Tate, Avery and all of us were put in extreme danger by one of our own.

I turned my attention toward Vito. "Everyone needs to be interrogated and questioned to make sure we don't have any other moles."

Vito thinks on this for a second and then nods his head. "I'll get a group of guys that I trust, that we both do, and I'll have them start gathering people up. We could finish interrogations today."

Vito smiles right before he looks at me, "I just had a new lie detector test delivered. Torturing methods are getting somewhat messy. Maybe I've been doing it for so long I'd rather just not. It's not fun anymore."

I stare at him for a second then burst out laughing. I try to stop because I'm afraid I'm going to offend him. Vito Romano is not the man I want to piss off. Thankfully he just starts to chuckle right along with me.

Everyone takes off to what they're supposed to be doing now. Most of the guards are in interrogations. And the ones that pass are helping interrogate others to move things faster.

I watched a little bit of the routine as it was happening. I couldn't stand sitting at my desk anymore.

Vito had an emergency call out for five more lie detectors. He was only able to get these older sets. They'd be delivered within an hour. Which works pretty well seeing how we have three-hundred and twenty-seven people to move through this process.

While one is inside a room being interrogated and questioned the others waiting outside are prepared with the stuff they need on their body and with how the process works.

With how fast they're moving, this should be done in a couple hours. There's no reason for me to be a part of this process, everything seems to be flowing smoothly. I'm tempted as hell to go up and check on Avery and Tate but one of the guards let me know that they both fell asleep. I know the girls are probably fuming mad with me right now, but I just need them to stay safe and put away.

I've got a lot of mindless shit work I need to catch up on. My biggest annoyance being emails. That's what I decide to spend the next couple hours doing.

I HONESTLY BELIEVED THAT EVERYBODY ELSE HERE WITH us was one hundred percent loyal. Vito squeezes himself through the partially open office door. As soon as I seen who it is, I get up from my desk and meet him halfway. I know he is here with the results.

"Out of three-hundred and twenty-seven employees we found two that have been wishing you harm."

"No way," I stammer. I've done everything for these people. "Who?"

"One person was for revenge, it was a maid. She's only been here for a few months. The understanding is that your father killed hers so she's here for revenge." Vito looks at me and I can tell he's feeling my pain. Yeah, this is eating me up inside and out. I decided when I first took over for the Mancini's that the loyalty of my crew was going to be bigger than anything. I would make sure that I always heard everybody, and that my door was always open.

"The other was a spy sent by the Irish." That one doesn't shock me as much as the maid. I wonder if I could talk to her. Vito must sense what I'm thinking and he shakes his head no. "Both of them were taken care of. They had to be tortured to get the info out of them. The maid lasted longer than the Irish implant." Vito smiles, too bad she was a traitor, it's hard to impress that man.

We both sit down on the couch, taking a break and trying to let the day's events soak in.

Now that the house is clean, it feels ten times better.

We need to figure out what comes next, but for now, we sit.

CHAPTER 6

AVERY

"Tate, wake up." Tate starts to growl, she's never been a morning person, neither one of us have. "Get up, there's a ton of commotion out there, something's going on. Please, I don't want to go out there by myself."

Tate groans some more, barely opening her eyes, making sure it's me. I've been awake for thirty minutes, ever since the noise from outside the door startled me awake.

I know something's going down, and it most likely has to deal with what happened yesterday.

Tate tries her best to quickly get dressed. I wait patiently for her over by the master bedroom door. I figured out earlier the commotion wasn't outside our door, it's mainly coming from downstairs in the foyer.

I'm just thankful that the fucking door isn't locked anymore.

"Get your guys in order, Lane, we don't have time for this shit." I can hear Mac growl at one of the other guards. I guess there's layers of guards. It runs like a corporation.

Mac controls all the guards. On my grandfather's side anyway. Doppler controls all of them on Asher's side, but Mac had been taking over for him since he's been gone. *Where the hell has Doppler been?*

Asher spots Tate and I at the top of the stairs when we finally made our way out of the room. The only thing we've been able to hear is the running of shoes and even the clicking of heels. Everybody's freaking out for some reason.

"It looks like they're packing us up." Tate leans over and whispers in my ear. Damn, that makes sense.

"Everybody gather around," Asher yells as he waits for everybody to make their way to the foyer area.

There's so many men and a few women in the foyer. People are standing outside the front door, others are down the hallway. Tate and I just mimic others and sit on the stairs. From here at least we can still hear everything.

"As you all know, Luca has found us." I look around the room in curiosity, but nobody seems shocked. "At this point in time he knows that we know, he's right down the road a few miles. For our safety we have decided to head over to the Romano compound in Chicago."

The chatter starts to go up a lot, to increasingly high levels. Both good and bad, these guards suck. I thought they were just supposed to smile and guard.

I can understand it, New York and Chicago are not close to each other and for most of the guys this is where their home is, where their family is.

"Our only goal for today is to make sure that we arrive there safely. Mac will get with each and every one of you about your location and area that you're working in. Some will go, some will stay. For our normal guards this will not be an option for you either way, you will all be stationed in Chicago."

I smile when I don't hear one damn noise, if your guys are whining about their job that's a big fucking issue, especially in this life. When it comes down to it; are they going to be too scared or whiny to stop that bullet that's going to go through your head?

"Even though it's still very early, at least the sun's starting to come up. The SUVs have been arriving all night. I know many of you have seen them already. There will be eleven groups of thirty people, each group will have six SUVs." Asher chuckles before he continues, "I know a lot of them look like shit, about ready to die. We had to go with what they have, and this will work a lot better."

Asher points in the direction of me and Tate. "The girls will be riding in one of the older SUVs. Not one that is going to crap and break down, but one that we wouldn't expect them to be in."

Tate and I look at each other with a worried look. We're both just going with the flow, right now we're letting these guys do their jobs. Asher gives me smile. I'm not the happiest with him right now for locking me in the room, but I'm worried, because I know he hasn't even slept at all.

"All lieutenants please get with Mac so you can find your assigned seating spot and car. The house is pretty much packed, only essential. We should be ready to go within the hour." Asher glances around making sure that everybody is paying attention. They are. "Let's get to it."

The guys start all shuffling and moving in every direction. Several were running but most are just walking fast. If they weren't ready, under an hour isn't very much time.

Tate and I both look at each other and then we both run back up the stairs, she goes to her room and I go to mine. We've both moved around too many times and lost a lot of our shit. I'll probably come out with one or two bags and my girl will have at least fifteen, she does love her clothes.

When Tate walks into the room in total black I start to laugh. "You look like one of the guards." She chuckles and then blushes a little.

I noticed in her hands that she has some clothes. "In a second you're gonna look like one of the guards, too.

They want us to dress more as a part of the guards. We'll be safer if we're all wearing black, it'll be hard to distinguish who we are."

She's got a point. I quickly take the clothes and change. They're a little big. I must've received an extra pair from one of the guards.

My doors opened and two men I've seen a couple of times, I don't know their names, run in and grab my luggage. I have one huge duffel bag and a carry-on. "Ma'am," one of them says, and they both tip their heads to me and run right back out the room. They probably have a shit ton of other stuff to do.

Tate and I make our way downstairs feeling like a couple of bad asses, because we rock these outfits we're wearing.

Asher starts waving us over once we reach the bottom of the foyer. Normally it should only take twenty seconds max in this huge colossal building, but it takes almost a minute to move around everybody making sure we don't get knocked out with bags or boxes. This place is freaking hectic.

Mac, Asher, Carter and one guard I've never seen are standing by the dining room door, all four of them are in their own little huddle.

"No," Tate whispers, she dramatically slows down while we're walking. I have to drag her with my arm practically.

I look over to see what she's looking at and her eyes

are pointed right at Carter. "I don't want him in our group, Avery."

"I know," I say. "This is the way they arranged it so this is the best way for us to get there safely. It's not that long. I don't think we're driving the whole way, there's got to be an airport nearby."

We both groan at that. Tate and I really don't like road trips that much. Not because it makes us miserable, we make whoever we're riding with miserable. One of us always has to pee or we're hungry, but of course never at the same time.

"You girls ready?" Asher asks as he wraps his arms around me. Tate stays slightly behind me, as far away as she can get from Carter without being too far.

"Yep," I gave him a smack on the lips and then go back with Tate toward the front door. We were warned not to get too close to it, because they don't know who's watching. I don't know what exit we're going out of.

"Maybe we could trade Carter for your grandpa?" My eyebrows raise up. I wouldn't mind if my grandfather was in there with us. I start to look around for the old man, but I can't find him anywhere.

"Have you seen him in a while?"

Tate shakes her head no. "I heard one of them say he's in Chicago right after Asher's speech. He's probably there getting it ready for us."

I nod and release the breath I was holding. Now I'm

not gonna freak out for however long it takes us to get to Chicago.

We follow Asher and Carter over to the garage doors. That makes sense, I think to myself as I watch six SUVs pull into the garage and close the doors.

"Over there," Asher points to a red Ford probably made in the '90s. Looks in decent shape and the windows are tinted.

Tate and I squeeze into the back while Carter and Asher squeeze back in there with us. The guard I don't know very well drives with Mac in the passenger seat.

This all makes a little more sense, not that many people recognize Mac as opposed to Asher or even Carter. Carter is the type that just comes and goes as he pleases. I don't even think he needs to be here. I just think he does it for Asher, there's no reason he has to do any of this.

"Where are we going?" I ask to anyone who'll answer. All eyes snap in Asher's direction waiting for him to answer.

"Vermont," he kisses me on the forehead. At least I'm able to sit next to him. Vermont, not even that far since we're right next to it, we don't even have to go south down by Manhattan.

Once we're done, we pull out and get in line with the other groups of waiting SUVs. They're still filling up more people and more cars so we shouldn't have to wait long on the side of the road.

I really want to ask what's going on and how they're going to do this but now I'm excited.

Within thirty minutes, everybody starts to make their way down the main road to get to the highway. They wouldn't tell me exactly where Luca's located, but I know it's got to be somewhere here. The Mancini compound is the end of the line for the road we're on.

Asher and I are way in the back. I don't wanna look around too excitingly, I need to make myself more unseen. I know Tate is thinking the same thing, as she pushes her body against the window and sinks into the back of her seat. She probably did the former, because Carter happens to be sitting next to her. Those two are as far away from each other as anyone can get.

When we get down to the highway everybody starts to take off in different directions. Three sets of vehicles go to the left. Three sets of vehicles go to the right. Three sets of vehicles go forward. I can't see the groups behind us, and I'm not sure where those went way in front of us.

We're the second set of vehicles that goes to the right. And according to the guys we should be to the unmarked airfield in under two hours.

The set in front of us gets off at the exit taking them down to Manhattan. We continue forward.

In the next thirty minutes is when we slide to the right and take the off ramp that leads us to another major highway.

The second set keeps going straight.

I watch the roads off and on for the next ten minutes. There's a black town car that's been following us ever since we made our first turn off of the road.

"Asher," I whisper and he gives me a weird look. "That town car has been following us ever since we left the house."

"I know," he says and wraps his arms around me. I guess I should be relieved that he's not worried. This is predominantly his main job. Being a boss sucks.

I lean into him and I don't say anything. He doesn't even say anything, either. This is all I need for comfort right now.

We travel for another twenty minutes. Every time I try to look behind me Asher turns my head straight forward again. But I did catch a glimpse and the guy is still there.

"Is Vito in Chicago?" I ask Asher and he nods.

"We got a lot of people coming in. I think he wanted to make sure his stuff is together." I nod. I find it a little strange, though. I know my grandfather has people for everything. Maybe he's hiding something. I shake my head, now my thoughts are going all over the place.

The longer we drive the more removed everything becomes around us. Fewer warehouses, fewer cars and fewer people. Not trees, though, the trees are every-where and they're so beautiful.

I'm almost to sleep when Asher snaps loudly. "Now!"

Asher grabs me, yanking me into his body holding me tight, painfully tight.

Carter does the same to Tate. She tries to struggle and push him away, but it's of no use, he overpowers her instantly.

I'm terrified and so is Tate as we both look at each other. How did the guy suddenly turn on us?

The car yanks violently to the right barely making a side street. Asher's grip on me keeps me from tumbling around in the back, the same thing for Tate.

We do a sharp turn again, this one to the right. The driver slams on the brakes. Asher, Mac, Carter and the driver all jump out of the SUV and run to the end of the tree line that we parked behind.

I can hear another engine, which was likely the town car from before driving fast spinning gravel, and just making an awful humming noise.

Less than a few seconds later the guys start firing. The town car explodes in glass, metal and screams. *Where are the rest of our people?* Maybe Luca's guards figured out that we were in this car, fuck.

"Tate, where are the rest of the guards at?" She scratches her eyebrows and then we both start looking through all the windows. The shooting has stopped outside and the men are making their way toward the car.

"There," Tate says and points to an area that's got to be at least a mile away through the trees. I can see a bunch of different colors of metal. And those are the same colors of the SUVs that we had earlier.

The men start walking back to us and quickly get into the car. The car takes off fast, most likely trying to get us out of there.

Usually I would want to look, but for some reason I turn my head to Asher right as we pass the car. I don't want to see what he had to do or what could've happened to him or us.

"This was a good plan," Asher smiles as me. "I didn't have enough time to get guys together. I sent out orders for all the groups to get rid of the men trailing them."

I smile, that was actually smart. I don't like what will come of these innocent men, but can they really be innocent if they're working for Luca Delano? *No.*

When we finally pull up to the Romano compound later that night, my mouth pops open and stays that way.

Tate smiles as she comes up and wraps her arms around me. "We made it, Avery, this is your blood estate."

My head snaps in her direction, she starts laughing. She probably spent the whole day coming up with that.

Doesn't take a long time to turn my attention to the

biggest fucking log cabin I have ever seen in my life. It's gorgeous.

Like a soldier not even paying attention, I immediately just start following everybody into the house. My head snaps back-and-forth. When we first enter the house, it smells absolutely divine. Different scents fill me. The fresh smell of wood is overpowering. I inhale as my head keeps looking back-and-forth. I imagine I must look like a snorting pig.

The walls are wood, there's beams that are wood. There's fucking wood everywhere. I always thought that would annoy me but it doesn't, it's actually beautiful and homey.

There are rugs everywhere, too, there's even one that looks like a giant bear. I want to ask if it is, but I'm not going to. The leather couches look like they're at least one-hundred years old, but it's most likely designed to be that way.

When I enter the kitchen I swear my heart stops. At least everything's making a little more sense now.

A couple of months after I arrived at the Stone's house, Arya asked me if I liked any of the countertop pictures she was thinking of. One of them was red oak, it was fifteen thousand a slab. Absolutely gorgeous, but holy shit, this is a magazine kitchen, it's beautiful. I can't stop rubbing my fingers over it.

I turn around and find ten people watching as I go through the house, one of them is Vito.

My head drops down quite fast realizing how

stupid I must look. I imagine I look like a tomato right now.

I quickly shake it off and walk over and give my grandfather a huge hug. "This place is beautiful."

He gives me a tight smile. His eyes shine with sadness and sincerity. "Your grandmother loved it. We've been working on it for a long time. I rarely ever stay here. I'm always working and on the move."

Tate whispers in my ear to go explore. I grab her hand as we go to search through everything. The only rooms that aren't totally covered in wood would be the theater room and several of the bathrooms. It balances it out some, I guess.

This place is probably only half of the size of Asher's, but it feels so much more welcoming, comforting. I love it here.

When I reach the top of the stairs, I rotate and look at the winding wooden staircase. Vito calls out for me, "Avery."

Tate and I walk over in that direction and enter the room that he was standing in.

"This was your mother's room, and it's only right that it's your room now." I wrap myself around Vito's side as we start to walk through the room. The roof must be at least fifteen feet tall in here. There are beams up at the top and the rest of the ceiling is painted white. Pine is decorating the walls and my room has a huge canopy bed that looks like it was handmade from the wood on the land. I chuckle to myself, it looks that way, but it was probably bought for ten thousand at some ridiculously overpriced store.

"This will be yours and Asher's room." Vito moves away from me and looks at Tate. "Let me show you to your room."

"Thank you," she says and I know she means it. We are all fucking exhausted, the only thing we wanna do is crash.

I watch them walk out and that's the first thing I do, lay on the bed. I should get out of these guard clothes, but I'm too freaking tired. It only takes several minutes before I'm out cold. A hurricane wouldn't even wake us up after the day we had.

CHAPTER 7

LUCA

No, no, no. Fucking Rocco is a god damn idiot. I get up from the makeshift office in this house and start to pace. That dumb fucking idiot. He ruined everything that we've been doing for the past six months.

Imagine my surprise as their going over their weekly meeting about all the shit that's coming up. Most of it I know because they go over the same shit over and over again. I'm shocked when the office door slammed open and Rocco was forced in.

I can't figure out what that idiot has done. I listened for a while as I watch him spill everything. It does not take long for that guy to give every inch of information away.

Doesn't take long after that for all of the audio devices to go off-line.

"Fuck!" I scream as loud as I can. Thankfully

nobody comes up and tries to talk to me now, they all know how I can be when I get like this.

Rocco has to be the stupidest person I've ever worked with, *ever*. He could've left a couple of audio devices. He didn't have to give every single one of them up. I imagine the Mancini's and the Romano's are going to do a thorough search, but not right away.

This is the second strike for Rocco. This is the end for him, the Mancini's will not give him another chance. Especially since Vito Romano is there.

When they first dragged Rocco in, I wasn't too worried at all. I like to take several precautions if I work with people, and that's to make sure that my name isn't connected to theirs. I never discuss work over technology. Always face-to-face, and it's usually with Armani. God, I have to call him.

Rocco isn't connected to anyone of us, my guys, through a cell phone. After I talked to Armani, I let him deal with his brother and what needs to be done. I just give the commands.

Everything would've been in place perfectly but then Rocco had to go and sing like a fucking canary. *Idiot.*

I'm disappointed in myself, not just these two fools I had working for me. I know better, but I was getting desperate. Desperate enough I would do anything to get Avery back to me, even work with the Mancini's.

"Seth," I snap. He's the head guard for all the men I

have around here. It's easier to talk to one guy and let them deal with the hundreds in place.

"Yeah boss?" He moves slower as he gets closer to me. My guys know that I don't have a very good temper. I don't blame him for protecting himself, but I really don't give a shit. Right now I want to fix problems, not cause more.

"Rocco gave up everything. I need you to head over there, take some guys. You're getting information, you're not trying to stop anyone or to snag Avery." I think on that for a few seconds. "Unless, of course, the opportunity presents itself, but right now we just need information."

"Got it boss." Seth winks, dumb ass takes off to gather his guys. I wish all my men were like Seth. I never have to explain simple directions. I know Seth will go grab several of our good guards and then they'll take off. They'll find out any information they can while remaining hidden. No one will even know that we're over there. Basically Seth is fixing Rocco's mistake.

They're going to start getting ready now. They're going to move out today. God knows where though.

I start pacing again, trying to come up with a plan. The blood coursing through my veins is boiling, that's how mad I am right now.

I noticed a couple of the guys glancing in my direction. After they would make eye contact, they would put their heads down just as fast.

"You, come here." I motion to one of the guys that is in the group, scared out of their minds.

"Y-yes boss?" God, my niece has bigger balls than this idiot.

"What is your name?" I would rather just call him guard, but I need him to work for me, and to work fast.

"Mark, sir." The young kid stands a little straighter as he tells me his name.

"Mark, start rounding up everybody. Have everybody pack their shit." I make sure to glare at him. I want to know that he's listening and he's not gonna forget half of the shit I said. "Everyone needs to be fully geared up and ready to go. We will move again, but who knows when it'll be."

"On it boss!" Mark says a little too enthusiastically as he goes to round up the guys. Hopefully they don't give him any shit, they saw me talking to him. Everyone can't stop talking and staring.

I can't say what we're doing next until I hear back from Seth. Rocco told them we were close by. We are about two miles away, the only place that I could find close enough to work.

———

"Hey boss. Seth is coming. We spotted him about a mile away." Mark nods at me, happy with himself, then turns around like a butler and runs out the door.

I stare at him for a second in disbelief, but at least

that fucker Seth is back.

I've been pacing this room for fucking two hours waiting for them to return, even though it's still daylight. They'll figure out a way to move Avery soon.

Seth finally makes it to the door a few minutes later. He walks in looking beaten and haggard.

"What the fuck happened to you?" I ask as I lean myself on the desk in front of me.

I don't think Seth was expecting me to snap out. He shakes a little bit and I bet if he had to pee right now, he would've pissed all over the floor. I need more good guys or loyal guards.

"We got stuck in a ravine close to the Mancini's house when all the guards were running around. It was the only place to go." My nose scrunches at that thought. He did come in smelling a bit ripe, but I don't fucking care. I need news.

I sit down right by the desk and let out a sigh of annoyance. "What did you find out?"

Seth takes another deep breath. "They're all running in different directions. Luggage is being packed, and the lead guard, I heard his name was Mac is yelling orders at everybody." Seth starts to ring his hands together, I can tell he is nervous. "One of the guys asked Mac if it was true they have to be out of there within an hour, and Mac nodded his head." Seth looks down at his watch. "That was thirty-five minutes ago, sir."

I stand straight up and slam my fist right on the

desk. The noise reverberates through the whole building, shocking some that are very far away. A small wet spot forms on Seth's black jeans. Making a trail down the inside of his pant leg and slowly dripping out right by black combat boots.

I clench my fists and look up to the ceiling. I'm not going to deal with this bitch right now. Looking back at Seth, I ask. "How are they leaving? What else did you see?"

Seth strains his back and stands at full height. He's acting like he didn't just fucking piss himself. "Multiple vehicles are being brought in. Dozens, we saw well over one-hundred. They were putting everybody in groups and it looks like they're getting everyone out that way."

That's unusual, unless they're doing it as a distraction. Normally they would get enough vehicles just to get out the important people. But if they're doing this, then that means they're getting a shit ton of vehicles and we won't know who's in what.

"Get the men together. We don't have that many vehicles, so you'll just have to pick who you follow. You can probably do this with twenty, use what they have in the other garage here. Some might need to be jumped. Stuff the cars full of guys and go after them."

"Got it boss," Seth says as he starts to run away toward the other guys. His voice changes; angry, darker and more authoritative. I smile again, relaxing. Seth is my right-hand man, but when he deals with me he just gets too scared. Maybe that's a good thing, at least it's keeping his guys in order.

Seth is taking all my guys that I have here. He left me with about ten, but thankfully I know how to fight. I'll fight with the guys if anybody comes here. Rocco never knew where we were located, he dealt with his brother and I dealt with Armani. Armani knows that if he let him in to all our secrets it would be the end of him. Luckily it's only going to be the end of his brother.

I take out my cell phone and dial Armani.

"Luca?" Armani says in a low tone. He knows I wouldn't be calling him unless it's an emergency. Like now.

"Your brother gave us up. He might be dead now or he will be soon." Maybe I should've eased into it a little bit but I'm not one for doing that. Especially when I need to figure out what the fuck we're going to do now, and how we're going to get Avery and get away. I don't want to have to deal with these fucking Mancini's anymore...

The other line is quiet. I swear I can even hear a sniffle. Armani knows not to show weakness to me, it'd be stupid if he did. I will use it against him. Maybe not now, but at some point.

"What happened?" Armani growls out knowing that there's no way out of explaining to him the stupid shit his brother did. I also know that it's just a waiting game for me now.

"He got caught spying at the office door. Which was totally stupid because there was a fucking mic in there. It's like he was trying to find something else." I take a drink before I continue. When my bottle of water is empty, I make my way over to the decanter the previous owners had. I have no idea what's in here, but it's been good so far. These people like their whiskey.

"They tortured him for a while. It didn't take long until he told them everything. They know your part in this and they know mine."

"Fuck," Armani growls out. I know he's in a shitty place. He just lost his brother and basically his family wants him dead now, idiot.

My family's a bunch of ruthless assholes, but they're still family and we all stick together. It was my parents' idea for me to go after Avery and her family in the first place. I chuckle a little to myself. I bet they never realized it would get this out of control.

"We're trying to track down Avery right now. She's at the house, but not for very long. In case they get away, I need you to find out everything you can. I'm not sure if you have anybody you can talk to on the inside. One of the guys that will give you something, anything. We just need a fucking location, Armani."

"Got it," is all he says before he hangs up. One day he'll be bowing down to me. Sure, we share the same rank within the families. Even though he's betraying his family, a rank is still a rank. It's a way of life for us.

One day I'm just hoping he'll be of more use to me.

Maybe he can fully leave his family and come work for me. I start to laugh, causing a few of the guys that are walking by to turn in my direction. That boy is done and been kicked out of his family as of right now. I'm sure he's a free agent. I guess I don't even have to acknowledge his rank anymore, he is family-less.

I manage to make my way through a glass of whiskey by the time I get any news from Seth and the guys.

The ten men that I have left here are just walking the grounds and pacing the house waiting for news just like I am. Making sure that we're not going to be attacked.

That was an excellent idea how Asher Mancini took everybody out in different vehicles. It's almost impossible to tell who's in which vehicle. I know now, I just need to be better. I will be better.

"Boss, boss." One of the remaining guards runs toward the office with the radio in his hand. "They spotted her."

I start walking toward the radio. Static is coming through before a button is pressed. "Luca is here," the guard says.

"Boss, we got her. She's in a red Ford, older model with tinted windows." It sounds like Seth is trying to catch his breath.

"Go after her," I snap. "Don't let her get out of your sight, and if you have an opportunity to get away, grab her and get rid of the others."

Nothing else is said as the guard walks back into the living room. I don't care who dies as long as they bring Avery to me. They can get rid of her grandfather, her boyfriend, her best friend, whatever. Everybody's got a fucking label and most are useless. The only important one right now is Avery.

"Shots are being fired." I can hear Seth scream through the radio across the room. "They're taking all of us out." Other radios are starting to chime in where my guards are being attacked. The remaining guards and I have formed a circle. We're listening to each guy as he tries to explain what's happening.

Instead of being followed, the Mancini's decided to fight back.

Blood drains from my face as I plop myself down in a chair. The rage is starting to consume me. I know it's going to go over, but there's nothing I can do about it. There's nothing I want to do about it.

Avery has abated me again. These fucking men I hired were not able to get her, again. My rage is through the roof. I'm shaking, that's how mad I am.

Both of my guns are out in both hands as I start aiming at the guards that are currently talking on the radios, frantically figuring out what to do.

As soon as I hit three, the screaming starts and that's when they start to run. This is my element. This is what I'm good at, *hunting*.

I shake my head and smirk, which actually calms me down a little bit. My life is not worth anybody else's, and if a man is running screaming and crazy after me, I'll be firing back. None of these little bitches do that, they all run and hide.

I saw one hiding in the bathroom shower. A grown man, in the fucking bathroom shower. I shot him multiple times.

I spend less than five minutes going through the house and taking out all ten guards.

If any of my other guards make it back alive, they'll be taken out, too. They haven't been able to do anything I've asked of them, every single one is a fuck up. *A waste of space.*

I put my guns in the back waistband of my pants and head up to my makeshift room and start to pack. Nobody's coming back to this house, the owners are gone, and all the guards are gone. *Nobody.*

The rage is still seeping through my veins wanting to make me just kill more, do more, fight more. It's ridiculous right now because if I don't get my shit together and get out of here, I'm going to be just as dead as all these other worthless asses.

Now it's time for me to rebuild. New men that are worth my time and money. That are loyal and know what the fuck to do.

For now, I think I just need to pay Armani a visit. Him and his brother are the reason that everything went to shit. I know he could be useful later, especially by finding me excellent guys. Not anymore.

It's time for a fresh start.

CHAPTER 8

Avery

"There's my girl," Vito says to me as he comes into the library next to the recliner I'm lying on. This has been my go to place ever since we've been here. Even though it's only been about a week. I just love this room.

I tried to get Asher to bring all our bedroom stuff in here and just make this our new room, but he said no, of course. It won't be the library anymore if we were in here. It would be our bedroom, but it would be awesome.

"Are you ready?" Vito asks as he lays his hand on my shoulder. I nod my head and fold the fleece blanket that was on my lap. It's summer, but it's still chilly in this house. You can't get into a good book without a blanket and a comfortable spot to sleep in or read. I smile to myself as I loop my arm through Vito's and we start walking.

Today is the third day that he's been showing me everything. Every single room in the house has been gone over. That was the first day and then we started with the business. Accounts, so many freaking accounts. He does have an awesome ledger that explains everything involving the different accounts and what they're used for. Every single account had millions in it. It took a while for the gasps to subside, and for me to focus on what he was telling me.

I have no clue what I was going to learn today. I tried asking multiple times why he was showing me all this stuff. It's family stuff and some of it's cool to know but some of it I really don't give a shit about. Like the accounts and where money goes, blah, blah, blah.

We walk into Vito's office and he has me sit in his spot. He paces like he normally does.

In front of me on the desk are just folders upon folders of people. Vito doesn't say anything, I just start sifting through everything. I don't even ask, I'm curious, who are these people and why does he have folders on them?

Halfway down through the pile is when I land on the folder labeled Asher Mancini.

Vito smiles at me, "I have a folder on every key player in the different families. The top five families will get more information, everything I can find out. Some of the lower family members will have less information on them and that's only if they need to be included. Basically just the ones that give us enough trouble or shit. It's good to always have a folder for information on your enemies. In paper," he points to the folders on the table and then he points to the computer screen, "and in text."

Vito reaches down and quickly sifts through the folders then pulls out one that's named Luca Delano. "Luca isn't one of the top families, that's what this whole thing started for." The Delano's have been trying to get a seat at the table for years and that makes sense that my gramps would have a folder, especially seeing how he killed his daughter and son-in-law, and almost killed his granddaughter.

Vito bends down and looks me in the eye. "Always make sure you have everything you can on your enemy, more so than your friends and your legit businesses. There will always be somebody that wants what you have. That wants to take everything away from you, and you're not gonna let them."

Vito kisses me on the head and stands up to his full height and then walks out of the room. I know he's giving me a chance to understand all of the Romano's enemies, to look through these folders. I have nothing else to do today except sit in the library, but I find this kind of entertaining.

So I start. I even read Asher's and Luca's files in case there's information that I missed. Next, I go through every single other folder. Some of them shock me but not too much. It seems like every mob boss has a mistress, not really a shocker.

What's funny to me, though, is that I wonder if some of these mob bosses know that they're sharing the same mistress. A woman named Kitty pulls up on several of these pages as the mistresses of other high family members. Maybe they share. I laugh, I hardly doubt that even though they're cheating on their women, these men don't share anything, they just take everything they can, and have somebody else deal with the consequences.

I'm halfway through when a thought hits me. I don't know why it hasn't clicked for the past few days, maybe because I was excited to learn and see everything that was different.

Why is Vito showing all this to me? I lean back in his office chair and start to wonder. As a child, even a teenager you're not allowed to hear any of that shit. The doors are closed for a reason. I would be forced to go somewhere else. Not now, I'm going to be nineteen soon, but I'm still pretty young and still a teenager in their eyes.

What the hell is going on with my grandfather, and why am I going through all of the shit? I'll be honest, it's interesting to know the ins and outs of everything, but it's like he's grooming me to take over.

I can feel the unbearable chill, it starts at my center and bursts out through all my limbs making me so cold, I shiver. My grandfather is grooming me to take over the fucking family business, and I want to know why. He knows I don't want to do this and he knows I'm with Asher.

I leave the papers scattered on the desk, and jump out of my chair in a mad search for Vito. I could just call him and ask him to meet me in here, but I need to do this now, I need to see on his face what's going on. I need him to explain everything to me.

The thoughts are going through my mind, horrible thoughts, weak thoughts. Any sick shit that I can twist up in my head.

When I make it down to the foyer, I see Carter standing there talking with one of the maids, getting a little too close.

I interrupt because it's my fucking house, and I don't like him that much because of what he does to Tate. "Have you seen Vito?" I ask as I move right into their small space. The girl, Minnie, I think is her name, blushes and walks away. Probably embarrassed that she was caught with the devil.

"He's in the garage looking at the new cars they just brought in," Carter says and walks away. He gives me nothing else, not even a quick little smile. The guy is a grouchy ass, but Asher loves him to death for some reason.

I'm still determined to figure out what's going on, so I quickly make my way to the garage.

Vito, Mac, Asher and several of the guards that I

can't remember their names are standing next to a couple of black Land Rovers.

Asher and Vito smile when they see me walking toward them but their smiles falter when I get closer and they see my face. My grandfather looks a little guilty, but also extremely heartbroken. I make my way straight toward him, nobody else.

I don't even acknowledge Asher as I pass him. He doesn't say anything, he just watches with interest, wondering what's going on.

I lift my index finger, pointing at my grandfather. I'm opening my mouth for the needed air. He holds up his hand and says. "Let's talk in my office."

The way that he said it, mixed in with the fatherly figure of knowing that you're not gonna like what you're going to hear, but you're going to have to go through with it no matter what. The tears start to silently run down my cheeks. I'm not sobbing or shaking, but I just can't stop what's happening and I know exactly what my grandfather's going to tell me.

When we get to the office he has me sit on one of the leather couches and he takes a spot next to me. Both of his arms wrap around me and he pulls me to his chest and I just let the waterworks flow.

"I have stage IV colon cancer. They gave me about six months to a year. That was right after we got here."

A strange wailing sound comes from me. My eyes burn with fire as the tears manage to break free, faster now, not slipping out like before. I relax myself not fighting it anymore.

The sobs come out quick and ugly. I hope that my grandfather shut the door as he walked in here. I don't want everybody else to hear this. I need to do this. I need to do this for him and for myself, but I don't need everybody else in this fucking house to know what's going on.

He holds me as I cry and sob for the next ten to fifteen minutes. This life can't keep taking my family members. There's going to be nothing else left for me. I sure as shit can't make my way through this alone. Vito keeps handing me tissues that he has stuffed in his pocket. That makes me chuckle when I look down at his hand.

Maybe he knew this was going to happen soon, so he stuffed them in his pocket like an awesome grandma would do. I start to sob again wanting my grand-mother. Maybe Vito could beat this with all this money and go out and marry somebody, so I can have a grandma.

"A cure?" I managed to spit out before I start to cough. At least I have a little bit of a window as the tears recede, I can blow my nose and clean my face.

Vito shakes his head no, "they've done everything they could think of. There's no new trials or anything for as advanced as I am right now."

Vito's eyes shine with tears. I take one of the unused tissues, because a used one would be downright disgusting, and dab his eyes. He gives me a huge hug, his strength is still there. Wrapped in his arms I feel like nothing can ever get through to us again.

Vito leaves the office for a second to go grab me a bottle of water or something to drink. I just do what my mom told me before when I feel too much, it's overwhelming. I start taking deep breaths in and out, releasing them until I can feel myself relax. The next thing she taught me is to get up and pace. It'll let you do something with your arms and your head. Your brain will focus only on walking and moving. A much needed reprieve from crying your eyes out.

Vito comes back in and closes the door behind him. The sob breaks free. He didn't know what I wanted. He brought me in a bottle of water, a Coke, tea and a carton of milk.

I don't move closer to him, I just stare at him as I wipe the remnants of tears from my eyes. "You're prepping me to take over for you? That's what we've been doing for the past few days and that's what we're going to continue to do, isn't it?"

My voice catches in my throat as the sobs wreck through again. Nothing can ever prepare you to take over everything in your family, and the loss of another family member when you hardly have any left.

Vito nods slightly and goes and takes his place back on the couch, letting me get my shit together. I'm pacing faster now. These beautiful hardwood floors are going to have to be redone as soon as I leave here.

I sit on the couch next to Vito and he holds my hand. I don't say anything and neither does he. I don't say anything because I'm still processing all this. I'm still trying to get it through my head. I want to lash out, I want to cry more.

Vito is an awesome man, grandfather, human. He just sits there quietly and lets me deal with it. Eventually the tears dry up and the thoughts disappear, leaving nothing except for just an empty shell, that is what I think of myself now.

A familiar hand shoots out and grabs mine, lightly yanking me up. I'm pretty sure it's Asher. The scent of his cologne penetrates me. He wraps his arms around me and leads me up to my room, tucking me into bed and turning off the lights.

It doesn't take long until the sweet darkness takes me away, temporarily ending this insane nightmare.

CHAPTER 9

AVERY

Someone continuously knocks on the door. I've been able to ignore it for the past hour, people would come and go, knock here and there, and then leave me alone. When I woke up earlier, I got up and locked the door. I just want to be left alone to deal with my thoughts and how to piece this all together to where it makes sense in my head before I deal with everybody else.

The continuous knocking is driving me insane. I yank back the covers, ignoring the sports bra and basketball shorts of Asher's that I'm wearing. At least I'm dressed.

I stomp my way over to the door, this is annoying. I plan to spend however long it takes in bed till I can get through my head, so I can get over the shit.

I yank the door open. How dare they keep fucking knocking, knowing my world is turning upside down.

When the door fully opens and my eyes adjust to the person on the other side, I start to sob, just as loud as they do. "V-Vito," Tate can barely say the words she's crying so hard.

I'm such an asshole, this is killing other people also. I grab Tate as we both fall to our knees. My best friend clings to me, identifying with the unimaginable pain that I must be going through right now. Tate only has Asher left, so this hurts.

She lifts me up by the arm and puts me back in the bed and she spoons me from behind.

We both cry, ugly cries for a man that we both love, Vito Romano. Everybody loves him. He just has a way of getting under your skin. He might be one of the biggest bosses on the East Coast, but he's also my grandfather, and one of the sweetest men I've ever known.

For the rest of the day, I love the fact that Tate stayed with me in bed. Asher came in a couple times, but he would just look at us and leave. He knows I need this right now and I love him even more for it.

Even Carter came in, but I think he was more checking on Tate than me. Maybe he just wanted to know where she was, keep your enemies closer and all that.

Around dinner time that night my body forces itself

out of bed, but it was my stomach that forced me to get up. At least I feel dried up now.

My stomach is growling like crazy but I'm still afraid to go out there and see Vito. I need to calm myself, my head can't take much more of this crying.

I bypass the kitchen when I noticed everybody in their having dinner. I'm not being dramatic or trying to get more attention or whatever it is that young girls do. I just literally cannot cry anymore. I know if I see my grandfather I will break. If I see Tate I will break, because she will try to help me. If I see Asher I will break, because he will have no freaking clue what to do. I chuckle a little bit, at least he might make me laugh.

One of my all-time favorite things to do is eat with the guards and thankfully there's a whole other building that's dedicated just for the ones that are off duty or for dinner time and sleeping.

I haven't eaten in over twenty-four hours. My first smile reaches my face when I see Mac in the kitchen cooking and I can smell Italian.

Mac turns around and sees me, that's when my eyes fill with moisture again making everything look like a kaleidoscope. I rapidly blink away the tears.

Mac looks at me and then looks around. I know he's trying to get my mind off of it really fast, trying to figure out something to do. He looks worried and freaked like were about to be bombed. I chuckle because Mac is more scared of a crying girl than a bunch of men with guns.

He whispers in the ear of one of the guys, he moves toward me and gives me a hug. He pulls back right away before he gives me a chance to melt into him and let the tears return.

My eyes are closed when he pulls back. I want to open them but before I get a chance, something fluffy is stuffed in my hands.

"Sneaker," I coo to the little shit and he actually purrs. Maybe he knows that I'm upset right now.

I love him, I squeeze the furball and pet him, then he bites my hand and I drop him down. Three seconds of love from Sneaker is probably the most anyone's ever going to get.

No tears and I'm feeling better. I smile at Mac as he wraps his arm around me. "Come on, I need help with dinner."

I spend the next few hours with the guys. The guys that are off duty, anyway. Mac hangs out with us the whole time, but I swear he's on duty at night, he must just be here for me. We laugh and we play card games. It was fun, it was a great time. Mac keeps texting on his phone, he must be telling the others where I'm at. They're probably just happy I'm not in the room anymore.

"Thank you," I say to everybody as I'm getting ready to leave. It's two AM and I'm really tired again. I make sure to make eye contact with every single guard there.

These guys didn't have to do this. This was their day off and I imagine some of them are bored, but there's other things they could've been doing and they took their time to make me feel better.

I sniffle and just swallow anything that might make me want to start crying again. I wrap my arms tightly around Mac. "Thank you," I whisper in his ear as he gives me a tight squeeze.

"Anytime girl. Door's always open, if this helps you to relax some, you come and hang out with us."

I give him a nod and bend down and pet Sneaker. It's time for my ass to go back to bed.

I WOKE UP A COUPLE OF MINUTES AGO. I'VE SLOWLY BEEN trying to pry my eyelids open. That's what happens when you cry for a long time. The next day it feels like your eyes are super glued together with gunk.

As soon as I open my eyes, I see the very entertained face of Asher looking right at me.

"Good morning," I say as he bends over and presses a kiss to my forehead.

"How are you doing today?" I sigh a little bit. I don't even want to think about yesterday, I just wish it never happened.

"I'm better," I smile and I mean it. I am better, I say as I sit up.

Asher sits cross-legged right in front of me and

takes my hands in his. "You know that every big bad boss woman has a right-hand man, right?"

I nod, wondering where Asher is going with this, but I have somewhat of an idea.

"The right-hand man does all of the shit for the boss that she doesn't want to. Some bosses have the right-hand man do everything, kind of like a silent partner. Only around if needed to be." Asher smiles at me, yeah I know where he's going.

"When people try to find the right right-hand man, this is a person that they have to trust more than their own families. More than their parents, more than their blood." Asher speaks quietly, then is silent letting it all sink in and let my mind wander. I don't even need time to think who would be perfect for that job.

"Mac," both Asher and I say at the same time. He's not Romano blood or even close to looking like us, but he's practically been running a lot of the Romano shit forever, plus he's family.

"That could actually work." I look at Asher and smile. I know I can't let the end of the Romano empire happen with me. The business meant so much to Vito and my parents.

Asher presses his lips together and gives me a tight nod.

"You won't always be able to check with him. You have to start making some decisions on your own, Avery. This all comes down to you, baby."

I know Asher's main intention was to make me feel

better, but all of it is overwhelming. It just seems like too much right now, I want to leave and get away for a while and not even think about it. I don't have that choice right now with Luca and my grandfather's health. This shit has to be dealt with now.

"I love you more than anything and we will figure this out. It may not seem like it, but I know it's important for you to hold on to your family name and everything your parents and your grandfather work so hard to keep, everything that Luca destroyed."

I give Asher a kiss on the cheek and then get up and get dressed for the day. Normally our big thing is morning sex, but I'm just not into it today and he can tell, that's why he's leaving me alone.

But my spirits are lifted, I'm feeling better. It might not be what I want at this moment but this is my life and I need to take charge of it, or somebody else is going to do it, they might even take it away from me. Everything would be gone, which would be much worse than me in the driver's seat.

I HAD JUST FINISHED TELLING TATE EVERYTHING I'VE learned over the past few days. Not insider shit, she doesn't care about that, but everything with my grandfather, is what we talked about.

She knew most of it. I'm pretty sure Vito and Asher

had her come to help me yesterday. They had to tell her what was going on. Today I told her everything.

"I can't believe you're going to be the head of the Romano family!" Tate squeals. I thought she would feel sad for me just like I was. I want out of this life, I just want to be a normal girl. Go to college and not do anything else. I don't even know what else normal people do. I do know one thing, they don't have to fight for their life all the time.

I give her a weird look, watching her look through my eyes to the shit storm that is my life.

"You're going to be a Mafia bad ass," Tate tells me as she starts to pace looking back and forth between me and the room. "Nobody's gonna fuck with you. You can even start changing things for the good. Change the whole way the whole company operates." Tate's hands are flying in the air mimicking everything she's talking about. "You could take the jillions of dollars, whatever this company is worth and make it legal."

Tate's eyes gleam with determination as she plops down in the chair. The doors open to the library, but then they shut quickly after a guard looks in. The guys have been checking in on us all day. Nobody comes in and stays a while or even talks. I think they just want to make sure that we haven't ditched, gone crazy or flooding the house with tears.

Her thoughts at first were bullshit. I didn't even really listen to Tate because I don't have a business degree, and I'm not very smart in any of the shit, so I don't know how to take millions from the drug industry and put it into something legal.

There's a way, somehow. I just have to find it. I can do this, I can switch everything and make the Romano Empire a legal entity.

I look at Tate and smile. "The new Romano name will be based on how much it helps the community. It will be legal on every front. People will know us by how much money we make and not by how many lives we take."

Tate smiles and sits up straighter, she likes where I'm going. Asher and her both knew how to get me going in the right direction. To let me see the whole picture, not just the things I didn't want to see in the first place. Even though Vito has shown me a ton of shit, it's not even close to everything that there is to learn. Starting tomorrow morning, I'm gonna work with him on everything. I want him to show me the shit I don't want to see and know. He was just doing the easier stuff at first, now I need to learn the hard shit.

I laugh inwardly to myself. Most people are groomed all of their lives to take something like this over. I wonder if my mom was next in line. *Maybe.* When they're younger, they are taught the bad way. I'm happy I wasn't being groomed for the business since I was little. I bet Vito might be a little bummed that I'm the wrong gender. But who really cares as long as I'm getting the job done.

My grandfather told me he could go anywhere from six months to a year. It just depends on how his body reacts to the medicine and to the cancer. I hope it's a lot longer, even though I need to learn everything. I want us to spend as much time together as we can.

You rarely ever hear about families turning their businesses all the way around. It's going to be extremely hard, but we can do it. I have a team of great people that are determined and will help me.

I will take everything in this company, its people, its connections, its money, it's worth and I will twist it around and keep twisting until everything comes out clean and beautiful. *No more dirty.*

CHAPTER 10

ASHER

I look down at my watch, one that's been passed down through five generations of the Mancini's. The only person I've known was my father and he wasn't worth remembering but I didn't know any of the other people that passed this down. Maybe there was a decent Mancini generations ago, there hasn't been one for years.

Vito and I have been in back-to-back meetings since he found out he was sick. He has a deep and extreme love for his granddaughter. It's like he's holding on to life for her. She's the ultimate being, the one that would continue the bloodline of the Romano's, for Vito.

I don't know if I'm turning into a fucking pussy or what, but every time I even think about the man and what he's going through, my eyes want to tear up. I've never given a shit about anybody else before except for Avery.

This explains why all my time is pretty much been for Vito, getting his affairs straight so is granddaughter has less to do.

"I'm in love with your granddaughter." I didn't mean for that to come out but it's been hanging on the edge of my tongue forever and I needed to tell it to somebody. I should probably tell it to Avery.

"I know," Vito says as he glances up and gives me a wink, then goes right back to doing what he's been doing.

I chuckle a little bit. "We're going to have lots of little babies and their last names will be just Mancini," I say with a smile, but Vito's face doesn't return it. He goes slightly pale and fuck man, Vito Romano's eyes gloss over. I keep thinking, 'fuck' over and over in my head. *Don't do this man, don't make this awkward*, I shout in my head hoping Vito can read my thoughts.

Vito takes a couple deep breaths and shakes them away. We're guys, we don't have to say anything else. And this will never be told to anybody. I know how much he loves Avery and what he's going to miss, great grandkids. It fucking sucks that this man had to get sick.

Really fucking sucks balls.

I've never had anybody that resembled a father figure, grandfather figure, anything. But Vito Romano was that for me. I've learned so much from this man personally. So much about myself, not just the business aspects.

"Fuck!" I snap. Vito's eyes look up to me worried. My eyes gloss over.

I pace around the room. Fuck, I don't want to be seen this way, so I make my way outside the door. A quick walk should knock everything off that I'm feeling.

The day I found out how sick Vito was, I swear I lost a part of my soul, not just for myself but for Avery. She finally gained somebody that was important to her, now she's gonna lose him, too.

I researched as much as I could. I had Mac and a couple of the other guys help me but Vito wouldn't qualify for any of the trials. Nothing could be done for this rare type of cancer he has. There is regular shit like chemo and new FDA approved pills. I guess it's supposed to make everything a little better but it doesn't.

I calm my ass down enough to where I can walk into the room. Vito gives me a tight smile when I come in, neither one of us need to say anything. Guys don't usually work that way.

"The kids can be named Romano-Mancini," Vito says all the sudden, twenty minutes later with a huge smile on his face. "I should mention that to Avery."

I start to laugh and crumple up some papers and throw it at him.

The families know how this works and so does

Avery. They might not have the Romano name anymore but they will be Romano's. I'll make sure Avery and Vito know this. The old fucker's just trying to lighten my mood. *It's working.*

"Okay," I start to say as I look through the papers on my desk in the office. Vito is working on the other side of me. "I'm going to divide the families up between the guys. Me, Mac and Carter should be able to reach out to all of them. We're going to have some trouble with the Armenians and possibly the Irish. The Russian and Spanish families should be fine. I have the other guys set up to contact the smaller families, then this way we can make sure that Luca hasn't taken any of them into his spell, and they don't know where he's at."

Vito looks at me for a minute and then starts to nod. "They know that our families are connecting. It would be a good idea for them not to fuck with us."

Which is totally fucking true. There is no way I'm letting go of Avery. The Mancini's and the Romano's will join together, connect. I'm the strongest on the East Coast and Vito's the second. The two families coming together will make us so huge that we'll be impossible to penetrate. Which is exactly what we need.

I know the time has come for me to ask properly. We're always talking and joking, but I need to do this the right way, now, before Vito gets too sick.

I've never done this before, but it doesn't matter,

the only thing I can do for Vito is let him give me shit. I know he's okay with me and Avery together already.

"I'm gonna marry your granddaughter, you okay with that?" I spit that shit out before I even had a chance to really think about it and I cringe. What a fucked up way to ask for somebody's hand in marriage. I continue on my stupid escapade before Vito tries to stop me. "I'm going to do it anyway, but I would like your permission. I would appreciate it, and I know Avery would, too. She needs you to walk her down the aisle."

Vito's eyes start to tear up, making us both extremely uncomfortable. "What the fuck. Stop that shit before one of the girls comes in here and sees us both blubbering like babies." Vito starts to laugh.

"Of course you have my permission," Vito says with the sincerity that can't be matched by anyone else.

I relax. I don't know why but it was just so important for him to approve of us even though he already does. "Thank God, what's my dowry?"

I hold a straight face as long as I can. "It's going to be a shot in the fucking head." I start to laugh, not a full on laugh like Avery does but it's a good little chuckle and it lightens the mood.

I pull out my phone to send a group text to all the guys. We need to start dealing with this shit now. It's time to find out what the other families know. "Let's get started," I say as Vito and I both stand up. This game is going to end very soon.

MAC, VITO AND CARTER SHUT THE DOOR TO MY OFFICE as they walk in. Walker, Liam and Noah have been working on other odd jobs that I've assigned for them. Doppler and Devin are supposed to be helping them out but I haven't heard from those guys for a while. Everybody does their own thing and are called back when needed, if they can come.

I shake away the worry when I think of Devin and Doppler. Those guys have been with me for years, but haven't been around lately. It makes me a little antsy, but I know that they're both extremely loyal so I'm not too worried about it. Devin didn't follow us when we came to New York, and he's still not with us in Chicago. He's been working in California on some computer contracts that he has. He's always done work for us and helped us out, it's a bummer because he was freaking awesome. I could probably entice him if I kept pushing, but he's on his own jobs right now.

I look at all the guys. We've all broke away from everything for a couple hours to eat lunch and make phone calls. "Anything?"

I search everybody's eyes trying to find if there might be something, a spark of something, some kind of hope to hold onto, but they all shake their head.

Mac leans forward in his chair slightly crumpling the paper that he had. "Nobody knows a damn thing. I tried enticing them, but it's hard to know for sure since I'm not there with them."

Vito holds up his hand stopping everybody. "The other families know how big we're getting. They don't want to do anything to harm us, so if they haven't seen anything, then I'm okay with that. I'm pretty sure that they haven't."

All of us nod. Vito Romano has about ten times more experience in all this shit than we do. And that's not just including his age. He had to redo the whole Romano line, which led to the connecting of the other families. The others were killing too many innocents. They had to stop it before the cops at a national level, agencies with more clearance than the CIA, started to bear down on us.

I don't know what it was like before, but I've heard the stories from other family members in the Mafia. It used to be pure war zones on the East Coast. Thankfully Vito dismantled everything, because who knows if we'd even be alive now if things kept going the way they were.

I open my mouth to continue talking because we need a plan, as the office door burst open.

A very pissed off looking Avery and Tate stomp their way in.

"We have a right to be here," Avery snaps as she looks at the rest of us. Her eyes soften when she looks at her grandfather.

All of us snap our attention toward Vito. We might

be scary Mafia guys but scorned women are not our jam.

"I ain't fucking dead yet!" Vito snaps and is clearly annoyed by the girls barging in. "When we feel that you guys are ready, then you will be in the meetings. You're not gonna rise to the top in one day, girl, you need to earn it."

The rest of us are trying not to laugh, we've never heard Vito talk this way. I know he's doing it for our benefit and the girls, who are still standing there with their mouths open.

Nobody says anything for at least a minute as we all just stare at a very shocked and speechless Avery and Tate. Waiting for them to walk the fuck out.

Avery instantly blushes and then mouths sorry to her grandfather. When she turns in my direction, I give her a wink letting her know it's okay.

When the girls leave and shut the door, Vito chimes in. Looking at Mac he says. "Weren't you the last one in? You need to lock that damn door."

I can't stand it anymore and I burst out laughing. Vito Romano is one scary mother fucker, but he never talks down to anybody and this is just freaking hilarious.

Mac tries to keep a straight face as he gets up and slowly walks his way to the door shutting it, pushing on it to make sure it's shut and locks it. He stays in that position for a minute as his shoulders shake. The rumbles of his chest are silent at first, but then they get louder. All of us are starting to laugh. Vito tries to keep up with his angry façade, but it only lasts about two seconds till he joins in.

It takes us at least ten minutes to get out of our shit and quit laughing.

Carter clears his throat, he's the only one that wasn't laughing very much. His cold and dead eyes just stared at Avery's best friend Tate. Damn, that girl does not know what's coming. She definitely pissed off the wrong fucking Beckett. All of his family members are moody and psychotic. Carter barely needs anything to push him over the edge.

I refocus my attention on Carter when he starts to speak. "We had some seekers out. They went through and searched the grounds that Luca used. They searched the whole area and interviewed anybody that might've seen anything. They pulled surveillance cameras from a gas station that was a few miles away from the compound, nothing panned out."

We all are quiet now, the stuff with Avery and Tate long forgotten as we each pay close attention to what Carter's saying. We've been waiting for information on finding that dumb fuck, but it's taking a while.

"He lost all of his guards. He might have one or two more close people, most likely Armani." All of us cringe at that, my teeth feel like they're going to snap and I just want to start throwing shit.

"He up and disappeared. None of the other families know anything." Carter takes a deep breath. I can tell he's very annoyed with the situation but Carter is normally annoyed with just breathing. I'm close to pushing and stabbing him to continue but I know he needs to do it on his own. I don't want him to forget anything.

"He can't be too far, we would've seen something. Someone would've seen something. Unless we didn't ask the right questions. One thing I did notice is that we need to not just ask about Luca, we also need to ask about Armani and anybody else that Luca is close with. His right-hand man is named Seth."

Carter did make a really good point, we've probably been looking at this the wrong way. Searching for the wrong man.

I nod, that makes total sense. I look over at the guys. "Get back with the families. Ask about other people that Luca will be around." I glance over at Carter. "I didn't even think about that, thank you." He just gives me a tight nod, no smile, he looks pissed as usual.

Vito stands up and comes and stands next to me. "Also, we need to make sure that we check on our alliances. Make sure that nobody's going to swing the other way in favor of Luca."

The guys nod, at least they know what to do for the rest of the day. Everyone starts to make their way out of the office, then that's when it hits me.

I walked toward them. "Luca doesn't have men anymore. Even if he was able to find some, there's no way that they could truly be loyal. The lockdown is over."

I watch the guys to see how they feel. I don't know if anybody's going to reject this offer or try to argue with me but none of them do. Even Vito nods his head.

"There's no reason for us to hide anymore. The girls want to go to school, they need to be able to apply, even if they go online, they still gotta get their shit. We have more than enough guards to watch and keep us all safe. For everyone's mental sanity, we are no longer on lockdown."

I look over at Mac. "Make sure that everybody has a good rotation schedule. Keep us all safe and let me know."

"Will do," Mac nods with enthusiasm. "We got enough men and supplies, we're good to go." Thank God, I think to myself as I nod at Mac. It'll be good for all of us to be able to go outside and do things, especially for the girls.

We refuse to hide against this bitch anymore. He'll show his face soon and we'll be ready. Hopefully we can just find the bastard first, but I doubt if that'll happen. I don't think we need to worry that much, Luca will come to us.

Our lives have been on hold for too long, no more, we're done. It's time for us to start living again and to quit hiding especially from someone so tiny.

In the back of my head I'm always careful, but now I'll make sure we're safe.

"Carter," I yell. He's the first one that left and is already down the hall. He stops and slowly saunters back toward me. Like we have all the time in the fucking world, dick.

I smile at him. "Get something prepared for training." Carter gives me a weird look before I finish. "It'll be good for the girls to have some more training and some of the guys."

Carter holds up his hands to start talking but I quickly cut him off. "A lot of people here are trained in one area. It'll be good to multi-train in different avenues. I'm not sure how well the girls are trained. Tate isn't and Avery is not bad but she could use a lot more." I think on that for a second and quickly add. "Don't tell her I told you that, since she has been training for years."

Carter takes out his phone and starts typing on it, most likely notes from what I'm saying. "I want everybody in on this except for maybe Vito. The maids, the cooks, drivers, guards, the girls, anybody that lives and works here." Free training is usually awesome.

Carter keeps nodding his head as I talk. I glance down at my watch and notice the time, it's still early. "Get it set up as fast as you can and meet me back here. It's only early afternoon, so there's no reason we can't start today."

I DECIDED TO SET US UP IN THE BASKETBALL COURT. More level ground here. I chuckle to myself when I realize that Vito doesn't have a tennis court, the man is slacking.

Less than two hours later the guys managed to bring us around fifty people. There are over three-hundred people here at any given time. The amount of guards we have is astronomical, but it's worth it. Everybody's been through the ringer and we trust every single one of them. For some reason it's just family we can't trust.

Vito brings out a worried looking Tate and Avery. I walk up to my girl. "Hey baby," I say as I give her a kiss and a tight hug. She relents and wraps herself around me. Thank God, I was afraid she was still snippy from earlier and I don't want to deal with that shit now.

Everybody's crowded around. I know when the shift change happens, more guys will get word and more will join. You can never have enough training in this job.

Carter starts to organize everybody with Mac. Mac knows pretty much most of everybody's talents. It astonishes me that he has it in his head, he can tell their weaknesses and their strengths. He has half of the guys set up to start teaching, and the other half ready to learn.

Some of my guys are very well trained in knives. Some well trained in guns, all different types. And some of them are well trained in fighting. I noticed that that's the area that Avery is practicing in.

From my understanding she's been fighting just with her fists and her feet since she was a toddler.

I focus my attention on Tate who looks as pale as a freaking ghost. I start to laugh and I wave her over to me.

She takes a deep breath, making her eyes wide, showing me that she's paying attention and she's manning the fuck up. "Don't worry, they just want to give you the basics. Out of everybody you are the least trained but we want you to have something in case you get yourself in another vulnerable position."

Tate nods her head and awkwardly stands next to me. I get Carter's attention when he glances in our direction and I nod toward Tate. He's on her instantly, not even saying anything as he grabs her arm and drags her to another area so she could start practicing.

It sucks the Mancini's have never really been for training girls. It's the old way. Let the man take care of everything and they can just service. How stupid, a lot of the women died when we were attacked because they didn't know what to do. Some were tortured and raped. I've heard stories before from long ago. This is one thing that I want to continue doing, making sure everybody's trained, even the help. Most people won't refuse this because it's extra and it might save your life, especially in the world that we live in. The world that they decide to live and work in.

Everyone is just standing around looking awkward and Vito notices this. I was hoping they would dive in, but it didn't work that way.

"It's okay to practice," you could hear Vito's booming voice all across the court. "In fact, we recommend it. You've always wanted to learn a different area, then now is your time. Also, if you're really good at something, I would recommend that you try to teach others."

I can just feel the air relaxing more that Vito has given a pep talk to his guys. Fuck, I'm gonna miss that old man.

Once everybody gets situated and start practicing, I can relax and move toward Avery. More people keep coming back to the courts. Some are watching and some are trying to coax the others into working. Virtually all the maids, cooks, butlers, the help staff is on the sidelines.

They'll ease into it, I tell myself as I move to watch as Avery goes against Mac.

I smile, when everybody notices they all stop what they're doing and start to crowd around those two.

They both have their fighting positions ready; their legs are spread shoulder length and their arms are up. Like a wrestling position. They continue to circle each other until Mac makes a move. Avery is quick on her feet to slap it away and move.

A bunch of wolf whistles are heard and Tate shouts. "Go Avery!"

Neither one of them lose their attention, they're completely focused. Mac smiles right before he makes his next move, a roundhouse kick, that if Avery doesn't defend herself against, he might just knock her fucking head off. I step forward as Avery returns one of her own kicks, knocking Mac on his fucking ass.

I smile at my girl as she starts to crank her neck back and forth like the boxers do and run in place. She is good. Tate starts to scream and runs over and jumps up on Avery wrapping her arms and her legs around her waist. Avery's jumping as Tate holds on screaming and laughing. All the guards are hooting and hollering. Mac gives me a smile and a wink.

We both know there's no way in hell that Avery could take him. Well, I might have to change my mind on that after seeing that Avery seems a little rusty, but she does have some moves and that might save her later. Mac does have a little limp in his step. Maybe the fucker is giving me a wink to save face. I start laughing as I watch everybody scream and run around and hug Avery and Mac.

After about an hour, we have well over one-hundred people out here now. Twenty-five of us are currently teaching. Avery and Tate have moved over to knives. God, that should be interesting. I'm not as worried about Avery as I am Tate. Maybe she'll just become a knife wielding bad ass, but I doubt it. She's the clumsiest one of us. Carter catches my glance and I strain my eyes at him to make sure he knows, don't let the girls get hurt. I'm about ready to walk in and find them a complete set of armor, but I know they need to do this. Avery's had a good amount of training, but there's so much more she needs, especially to be able to fight off Luca.

I smile as I sit down and lean against the tree that's by the court. This is the first time in a while that we've had some peace and happiness in our lives. Vito sits next to me and hands me a beer.

Yeah, everything is going to be just fine.

CHAPTER 11

AVERY

As soon as Mac whistles for the end of fighting, my ass limps over to the grassy area next to the basketball court, and I fall like I haven't slept in weeks and I just found my bed. I am fucking spent.

We never had training this hard when I was younger, yeah my parents wanted to make sure that I knew everything. But never in my life have I felt like I wanted to die right after I was done. Shit, right now I'm praying for the end of this pain.

Someone walks up and blocks the sun, casting a shadow right over my misery.

I'm way too tired to try to move out of the way or at least move to the side to figure out who it is. So I just lay there with my hand over my eyes. I know as soon as I get up to look at whoever's there, they're going to move and the sun's going to hit me straight in the eyeball.

Fuck being whiny, but this hurts.

Vito starts to chuckle as he holds his hand out to me. "Come on, Avery. Let's get you some much needed water and food."

I extend my hand as he yanks me up. He might be my grandfather and a lot older but the man still reeks of strength.

We walk side-by-side as my mind wanders from the stories that I've heard. Ever since I was a kid, I've heard about how much Vito can fight. Apparently my grandfather loves to just use his hands and fists, that's what he's best at. If it came down to it, I know he'll use the guns and knives especially if he's trying to save one of us. I groan as we continue to walk. It's not that far, just to the side entrance of the house but it feels like it's ten miles.

"You need to make sure that you're well hydrated and fed before you start training or you're going to end up like this every single time," Vito says as he smiles. The perfect way to deliver a lecture without it being insensitive. I nod my head, he's right and I know it. My dumbass is trying to overachieve.

I know everybody's dealing with this because of me, if Luca wasn't coming after me then we wouldn't have this problem. I needed to show everyone that I'm not this weak little being that they have to save. I need to earn my keep around here, especially the respect if I'm going to take over. Nobody has to stay here, but I know they will for a while out of love for my grandfather. I just pray that respect can pass down to me, and in return they'll take care of our shit and keep me alive.

As soon as he sits me down at the kitchen table I can actually feel myself starting to relax, maybe laying in the grass helped.

I can feel the swishing of Vito's hands, he's telling the cooks to whip up something.

A bottle of water and lightly buttered toast are placed in front of me. I mumble out a thank you and scarf everything down, including the bottle of water.

Instantly I'm already starting to feel better. If my old trainer could see me now, he would make it ingrained into my memory to not let myself get so dehydrated.

I actually feel really bad, like everything he worked with in training me, I just ruined it. I let out a sigh of relief that my old trainer is not here to give me shit.

My grandfather gets a hot cup of coffee and then sits next to me at the island. I watch as he calmly sips here and there while the cooks keep bringing me food. I didn't ask for it, but I sure as shit won't reject it. They're bringing me simple and bland stuff.

I finished four pieces of toast and now I'm on some gritty soup. I think it's clam chowder but I'm not sure, it's so good I don't care.

I've been wanting to talk to Vito for a while, it's been in my head there's just something that hasn't made sense to me. Since both of us are sitting here with no other distractions, besides some of the house staff, there's no time like the present.

"How come you never had a right-hand man?" Vito stills for a second as he takes a drink of his coffee. It's like the wheels are turning in his head and he's letting the question sink in.

"I don't trust anyone," my gramps clears his throat and takes another drink of his coffee before setting it back down. "My father and my grandfather had one but it was my grandfather's who turned on him, shot him straight between the eyes. Tried to take over the East Coast before my father ended him."

My mouth was slightly open a little bit in shock. That means that my great-great grandfather was knocked off by his right-hand man. That doesn't leave a good feeling inside me, actually leaves a shitty one.

"I always thought it better to have several men I can trust. It's worked well for me all this time." My grandfather gives me a smile before he goes back to sipping his coffee. Even though I'm gonna ask, I have a feeling he already knows my intentions.

"Would Mac be a good candidate?" The words are so soft when they come out of my mouth, it's like I can take them back if they don't feel comfortable anymore. I don't know why I'm so nervous, we're just talking. I know that it probably hurts my grandfather to talk about me taking over when he's still in charge and he's still alive.

"Mac would be an excellent choice." He smiles a little too big, letting me see all of his pearly whites. For a man of his age he has really good damn teeth. My grandfather's being a little too devious and playful right now.

I'm kind of stumped for words. I'm not exactly sure what to say because he's acting a little strange, maybe the medicine is getting to his head. I don't see how that will happen, because from my understanding he rejected all the medicine.

"We planned it that way. Even though Mac has no idea, I was hoping he'd be the one you would choose." My grandfather squeezes my shoulder and then goes back to smiling and sipping his coffee. I still rarely drink the shit, but it smells wonderful. I exhale the breath that I was holding in. It wasn't quiet, either, so I know my grandfather heard, his slight chuckle tips me off.

I smile to myself, Mac is my right-hand man. This is going to be awesome and epic. Shit, I just hope he agrees.

I angle my head to my grandfather and he smiles again. My mouth starts to slightly open as he holds up his hand. "He would love the position."

That's all I needed to know. My grinning is infectious, just like my grandfather's. I wrap my arms around him and squeeze, standing like that for a few minutes, my energy is not allowing me to sit down in my seat anymore. I'm too excited by all the possibilities of what's to come.

I would lose it all in a second, though, just for my grandfather to be okay, he knows that and so does everybody else. But one thing's for sure, I'm not gonna sit here and be in denial after everything that's happened in my life. People can leave you in an instant, so this time I'm going to prepare like he's helping me to.

I'm also going to pray. Even if we only get four or five more months as per what the doctor said, maybe, just maybe, he can squeeze in a few more months, maybe even a year. Of course my main goal is that the cancer just goes away and there's no more problems, but I'm not an idiot, and I've lived in this life long enough to know there's not much anyone else can do. From now on we need to deal with everything as it happens.

Vito slightly turns in the chair and angles his body toward mine. He grabs my hand in a comforting and sweet way. "Mac knows the ins and outs of the business. When I found out that I was sick, we bumped him all the way up. He's in all of our meetings and knows everything that's going down. He will be perfect, loyal and trustworthy for you."

I smile big, the same time the tears start to come down. "You've thought of everything." That's all I manage to say before I start ugly sobbing.

Vito being the superb human being that he is lets

me cry as he holds me. I know deep in my heart that Mac is the perfect guy to pretty much run the business for us. I just hope he feels the same way. Vito brought him in because he was sick, but I'm not sure if Mac knows exactly why.

I SPENT THE REST OF THE AFTERNOON IN A COMPLETE daze wandering around the house. I get to do things I missed doing as a kid, growing up and being at my grandparents' house. *Snooping.*

As a child I should've known every nook and cranny of this beautiful cabin. Since I never had that option, I'm learning it now.

It's not one of those extremely older places where there's most likely a tunnel or a pathway or even a room that you haven't found. I'm not even sure Vito has done that, when you need a place to store all of his important documents besides his office, besides a small safe. You never know when the bad guys are going to break in and want to look at everything or just destroy it all.

This is something I might ask Mac or even Asher. It breaks my heart every time I need to do this with my grandfather. I know it needs to be done. But it just feels deep down in my soul like there's never going to be enough time to go through everything, we're just trying to get through the basics and anything that might be important.

"Avery," Tate says. I can see her jogging to catch up with me. "What are you doing?"

I smile at her. I should've went and grabbed her right when I started this little adventure. She's the perfect person for it.

"I'm snooping. I couldn't do this shit as a kid, so I figured I should probably learn where everything is now. Even the stuff they don't tell us about."

Tate's face morphs into one of glee as she jumps up and down clapping her hands. *Perfect partner in crime.*

Together, if there's something to be uncovered in this house, the both of us will find it, hopefully.

Twenty minutes later and we're on our fourth bedroom snooping and giggling. Even though we're not finding anything, the fun factor is still pretty high.

Tate asks me. "Have you decided what you're going to do yet?" She turns around and it looks like she's pointing to the room, but she's actually mimicking the whole house. "What are you going to do about everything?"

Tate applied earlier to the colleges in Northern California and she was accepted into one of the most known and accredited universities. We screamed and cried, I was so happy for her. My grades are okay but not enough to get me into a decent college. I'm not sure if I even want to do that right now.

"I think I'm gonna apply to the community college for business. I can do it online, and it's only a two year course." Tate starts to nod her head, at least I got somewhat of a plan. "I need all the freaking information I can get, especially if I'm going to turn everything around."

I grab her hand tight as we start to walk. Tate's going to leave around the beginning to the middle of August to set up her stuff and get ready for school. I'm gonna miss her like freaking crazy.

The thought hits me again that my grandfather's leaving and never coming back and Tate's leaving, too. I'm taking deep breaths as I pretend to look at something on one of the spare bedroom's dressers. I do everything in my power to shake these thoughts away right now, I can do this. I have my grandfather right now and I want to take time hanging out with him. Plus, Tate's going to be clear across the country, but she's still here, right now. I just hope to God that she comes back to the East Coast later.

Tate and I finish thoroughly going through another room coming up completely empty again. "This house blows, there's no cool things."

Tate starts to giggle. "When you and Asher have children, you guys really need to do something here and make some hidden pathways and shit like that. This house is too big not to be exceptionally cool for children."

I nod my head very dramatically, totally agreeing

with her. Yeah, there needs to be more cool shit in here. Maybe like a movie theater.

Both of us are getting ready to go into another room, one that I haven't seen on this floor even. Commotion toward the front door snaps our attention in that direction.

We don't have that much else to do besides snoop. Tate and I look at each other and smile, we both know what we're doing as we walk down the hallway toward the stairs. There's a perfect view at the top of the stairs that lets you look over the foyer. It gives you a good view of the beams and you could see all the wood that sprouted around. It's absolutely stunning.

I look down below and watch as the guards bring in vase after vase of white roses in different states of decay.

"What the fuck!" Tate snaps as she grabs my hand and starts dragging me down the stairs.

These flowers are not beautiful at all, they're dead. The vases that they come in are pretty, but that's about it.

The guards stack the flowers in every area they can reach. There are nice little end tables set out through the foyer plus glass tops located here and there. Too much if you ask me, but rich people need places to set all of their rich people shit.

"Just set it on the floor," I say as they keep looking for places to put the never-ending vases that are coming in.

Tate has been collecting all of the cards in her hand, moving from flower to flower. When she is almost done that's when the foyer fills up with more guards including Vito, Asher, Mac and Carter.

Asher comes and stands next to me in a defensive position just making sure I'm okay. Vito comes and stands on my other side, while Carter moves close to Tate and takes the little notes out of her hand. She goes to snap at him but then shuts her mouth when she sees the rest of us watching. Even though he's being a good little asshole bringing the notes back to Vito.

Asher snatches the notes out of Carter's hand. I can feel his demeanor as he gets more intense and more pissed the more he reads through them. Vito's not looking, he's walking around the different flowers, which there has to be at least one-hundred vases of twelve-dozen roses. That's a lot of fucking flowers.

I can tell at first that Asher doesn't want to pass over the notes. I poke him in his side multiple times before he stiffly hands them to me. There's about twenty or thirty guards, plus us in the foyer all staring at me wondering what the fuck is going on and why someone would deliver dead flowers.

We all know who it is, but it's better to not take a chance.

You're dead to me.

No longer a conquest, but a competition.

Soon Avery.

I plan on burying you, right next to your parents.

Your mom was a screamer, wasn't she?

We could've been beautiful together.

The tears start to fall and Vito snatches the cards out of my hand, reading them aloud. Shit, I thought that's what I was doing, but I guess I wasn't, I was just quickly sifting through them, letting Luca's hatred consume me.

"Fuck!" Vito Romano roars, scaring the shit out of all of us. Even Asher and Tate jumped. My grandfather does not roar, my grandfather's not one-hundred percent himself at this time. It had to be soul crushing for him to read those things about my mom, his daughter.

In the short amount of time I've known him, I've never heard him yell. Arya and Garett always said that he was cool, calm and collected, especially when dealing with work.

He stomps away and all I want to do is go after him and make him feel better. Asher grabs my hand and pulls me to his side, not letting me move.

I'm pretty sure I have the answer, but I need to make sure. "Does this mean what I think it means?" My voice is so soft as I speak to Asher through the angry cries and promises of revenge from my guards.

Asher nods, pulling me into a full embrace putting his mouth down toward my ear and whispering, "Luca Delano now thinks of you as the enemy, like he did before. When Vito Romano passes away, that makes you his huge competition. You will be at the top of the food chain so to speak, the place that Luca has always wanted to be."

Asher rubs my shoulders up and down as I take in this new information.

I nod my head as everything makes sense now. The Romano's are a more powerful entity than the Delano's and even if we come together, I would still be in charge. He would have to physically make me do what he wants and that won't be possible with all the guards, especially with Mac as my right-hand man. The only viable option for Luca is to kill me.

I glance at Mac out of the corner of my eye. My heart feels a little lighter as I watch my favorite guard yelling out orders getting guys to move. Several of the men had chased after the flower truck delivery driver just to get any information they can. Every little bit helps, maybe Luca messed up and we can go right back to where he's located at. But I doubt it.

I can't pinpoint how I'm feeling. I mean things are better, but I know that if Luca grabbed me right now he's not going to kidnap me and take me away where he could rape me and make me spit out babies. No, if Luca grabbed me right now he would put a bullet in my head. I feel relieved but also more angry and scared. I didn't get this far and work this hard to get a bullet in my head because Luca can't figure out the right way to get up to the top without killing everybody, or listening to his useless parents.

"Meeting. Everybody," Vito shouts as he stomps his

way back into the foyer. At least he was able to take care of what he needed to do.

I had a feeling this time we would be invited, especially if we wanted to go in and listen, but I don't want to. My grandfather is rightfully in charge now, and I don't even want to go into that meeting and hear any of it. The same shit we've been dealing with for over a year.

Vito comes up and gives me a hug, more of a silent apology of him overreacting. He leans down and whispers in my ear, "Luca is dead."

Those were the words I needed to hear, especially coming from him because I know that's going to be our main focus from now on, putting a bullet in Luca's head before he gets to us.

For the next two weeks my mind has shifted to match everybody else's, fight mode. We are at the point in time where we need to figure out how to end all this madness, so that we can move on with our lives. Everybody is retrained, and if they're good enough in some areas, then they're trained in others or used as teachers.

Poor Tate is miserable, but I work with her every day and we bust our asses.

This is what the guys had their meeting about. What they wanted us to do, train hard for two weeks. Tate shocked us all by becoming really good with knives. Now she has them strapped to her thighs and she looks like a freaking badass.

Everybody in this house is deadlier and more trained than regular guards, not because we know how to use everything and we're undefeated. No, because we have heart. All of the guards were busted up over how sick Vito Romano is. His team is loyal and true, they would lay down their lives for him. Which is more than I could say for whatever guards that Luca might have.

A week after Vito made the announcement that we're going to be excessively training, they started calling the Delano's, seeing if they can talk some sense into them, by getting their son off our backs. From what Asher told me they were worse than Luca himself.

Luca needs to die, and I agree 100% with them. I just kind of wish I could do it myself.

I want all of this over so I can spend the last remaining months that I have with my grandfather. It might not even be months anymore, it might only be weeks.

My heart breaks more every day. A piece of it shatters every time more shit happens or someone else is taken away from me. I'm sick and tired of losing everybody, *no more*. I might not be ready but I'm fighting back like a mother fucker now, it's time to put this thing to bed, and Luca in the ground.

CHAPTER 12

Luca

The muscles in my arms are starting to shake as the chokehold I have is not as powerful as I want it to be. The guff's from the man that I'm currently sucking the life away from are starting to distinguish on their own, coming out smaller and softer.

I should feel some sense of remorse, something. But honestly I don't. I don't feel anything, I don't even feel better that this is done and out of the way.

When the old bastard finally relents, I get up and take a long pull from one of the thirty different fucking decanters the old man has. This just screams fucking alcoholic. I stand here and look at his stash.

I know he does it mainly for guests, because I barely had ever seen him drink in all of my twenty-four years on this planet. It doesn't matter, my father was a piece of shit and I'm glad it's done.

My mom on the other hand, hurt a little bit more than I would've liked it to, but not enough. She was there every time my father decided to beat me, whispering in his ear when he was trying to be nice. She's just as fucking sick as he is, probably worse.

A woman who would let her child go through that is a piece of shit, but a woman who would instigate it and let her child be the victim of beatings and other shit is ten times worse.

That's why Mama was sliced and diced. The only thing I wasn't expecting was my father to wake up and come down right after I finished. He got an eyeful of his wife. I was hoping to put a bullet in the fucker's head while he was sleeping, short and sweet. Not having to deal with them like this. Maybe because I respected the man more. The bane of my existence, the horrible way that I grew up. I know that my father had just a little iota of decency left in him, my mom has been depleted for years.

I will never forget the heartbreaking scream when he spotted the devil of my mother on the floor. Just an inner shell of her former glory. The cry that came from my dad, I'll remember forever.

I wasn't exactly sure how I would feel once it was done. I knew it might be a little hard to do this, because these people are my parental figures. I felt a tiny, microscopic twinge of hurt for my father and maybe for the mother that I didn't have. I know after being around other families and seeing how Avery's parents were with her, that my parents should've never had kids.

If I could go back to that time I wouldn't have listened to them. I still would've killed Avery's parents, but I would've taken Avery and left. Escaping to another part of the country far away from the Mancini's and the Romano's and the Delano's. Someplace far, where nobody could ever find us.

Do I regret killing her parents, not really, everything must come to an end, nobody's going to go on forever. They're just a stepping stone into getting the Delano name to its rightful place on top. It won't be with my fucking father, though, I'll be taking over the Delano family from now on. This is something I should've done before, but I quit. I thought maybe they would be useful later. They're not, these sad people that some might mistake for parents or pieces of shit that don't deserve time on this earth anymore.

I ended them both in the family room, that's close to the dining room and kitchen. This place makes my skin crawl. It's like a bunch of older people walked in the house and threw-up Victorian shit everywhere. There is not one comfortable piece of fucking furniture in this house. Everything is just for show, even though it's immaculately clean, it lacks any warmth and comfort, *just like my parents*.

I look around the room, eyes that are staring at me, some are mad, some are scared and some just don't give a shit. I'm looking for the ones that were loyal to my father. I want the ones that are going to be loyal to me into the future, loyal to Luca Delano.

"My father was a piece of shit," I yell out, my voice not too loud but loud enough to be heard. "I don't have a beef or issue with any of you, but I am taking over. If anyone wishes to leave, that's fine. If not, you're more than welcome to stay on and help me end the Mancini's and the Romano's once and for all."

I watch as everybody huddles, talking to each other. Some leave instantly and it looks like others are going to get their belongings. I don't really know what I can expect from this, but some loyal men would be awesome.

From what I have planned, too many men will just fuck up the whole situation anyway.

I walk over to my father's enormous bar this time, I pick up a glass and a decanter and then make my way over to one of those fucking uncomfortable Victorian chairs. That's the first thing I'm going to do when I get everything settled, remodel this whole fucking place, or burn it down. I'm on my second drink before the last of the men finally make their decision. I can tell I have less than ten, this will be the perfect amount.

I ended up with a total of seven guards and Seth that decided to stay on. Two of them are younger, most likely new guards, not sure what they're getting themselves into. The other five are older guards that have been with my father for years. This is the kind of respect I want. I want loyal men that will stay on. The younger ones I'll have to train myself. None of the damn house staff stayed, which I don't blame them, there's jobs all over.

I stand up, making sure to acknowledge all of my guys in the eyes. Shockingly, I don't have one woman left but after everything they witnessed with Avery, the women are bitches and they don't deserve to be part of my group anyway.

"Let's get to work," I say as I stand up and clean the coffee table off with one swipe of my hand. My mom's figurines and gross older shit shatter as it hits the hard tiled floor.

In my bag I have blueprints and a lot of notes that have been taken over the years by multiple people. The only thing that sucks right now is the fact that I have nobody on the inside.

I look around at everybody. "The only way we are going to be able to do this is with poison or gas. Their guys outnumber us about thirty to one, so this is our best shot unless you all think you can take on thirty guys each?"

The younger ones quickly shake their head back and forth looking at each other with wide eyes, as the older ones grin and nod. Yeah, those older guys might be loyal but they're fucking idiots. I have one shot at this and I need to make sure it all works exactly how I have planned.

I throw the notes and the blueprints on the table so that everybody can see. "At first I wanted Avery

Romano alive and out of there, but now she's the enemy." I shuffle my papers around until I can find a folder that has three pictures in it. "Asher Mancini," I say as I pull his picture out. I place the two that I have left right next to his. "Avery Romano and Vito Romano, these three need to die, and I want proof of their death. Bring their body back, bring their head back, whatever the fuck floats your boat."

My heart constricts a little bit and I know it's because I'm thinking about Avery. But this is the way things have to be done now with Vito on the outs. From the gossip that's going around, Avery's going to be the new head of the Romano's. Let's not forget the fact that the little bitch is shacking up with the enemy and those two are going to end up making one huge fucking alliance. One that I know I can't get through. This is my only chance to take out everybody that's keeping me from my rightful place.

"Let's get to it," I say as all of the guards get settled in and really start working on this plan. "Make it one that will actually work. We only have one shot." If we're not successful, we're dead.

JUST SHY OF SEVEN HOURS LATER. THE BOTTLE THAT I have is almost empty and the guards ordered pizza three different times. I can't believe how much these fuckers eat, I should start charging them. But then again, I smile remembering that I am the heir to the Delano's, and I can afford it. Ain't nothing going to happen. The previous employees of my father will never open their mouths. I will come after them if they do, I'll end everyone they hold dear.

All of us walk out to our vehicles. "We'll meet again in a few days, it's time to get this done."

"Yes boss."

"Got it boss."

"See you then boss."

This is the first time in over a year that I've felt that we actually have a decent plan underway to get everything fucking done. Time is gonna be on our side for once, and that's all that fucking matters.

I toss the last remaining gas can back into the house as I light up a blunt I've been holding onto for a while. I'm normally irritable all the time as it is, so when I smoke the shit, it adds to my irritation. I don't think it'll happen this time. I feel relaxed for the first time in years.

I wait till everybody's a safe distance from the house, driving away before I toss half of the joint that I've been smoking right in the doorway of the home I grew up in.

I hear the flames igniting while I walk away. I can feel the heat penetrate my clothing, going deeper until I can feel it in my bones.

There's no better way to start over, than to start over from scratch. I hated this house with every fiber of my being. I'm grateful that I never have to look at it again.

IT SUCKS, THOUGH, THAT MY PARENTS DIED IN A HORRIBLE FIERY HOUSE EXPLOSION. I CHUCKLE TO MYSELF FOR A SECOND, DÉJÀ VU, JUST LIKE AVERY'S PARENTS DID.

Seth and I both stand next to his Land Rover as we watch the flames touch and ignite different parts of the house. "Let's go," I snap out. Better to get out of here now instead of explaining everything to the authorities when they show up.

Soon, the whole kingdom will be mine, and all of this will be over.

CHAPTER 13

ASHER

The nudge against my right arm has me jerking my eyes wide awake. Vito Romano is in my fucking room in the middle of the night nudging me awake.

At first my fighting stance was in position, I was ready to knock a bitch out until I saw who it was. It could only mean one thing if he's in my room in the middle of the night trying to wake me up.

"What's wrong?" I whisper snap at him.

Vito doesn't say anything, he just glances from me to Avery, who was thankfully still passed out. He then glances from me to the doorway letting me know that he needs to talk to me.

Thankfully, Vito waits for me in the hall as I try my fastest to get ready. But everybody knows if you try to put pants on while you're half-asleep, your ass is going to end up on the floor. The good news is I'm much better than everybody else. I chuckle to myself as I walk out the door.

My body stiffens right when I walk out and I catch Mac and Vito with grim expressions on their face. I don't even get a chance to ask what's going on before Vito starts talking. At least we're far enough away from the door that we don't have to worry about Avery hearing or waking up.

"The Delano's were attacked last night. From the reports and from what we've been able to gather, they were dead before their house was burned down," Vito says. Something else is on his mind.

I keep rubbing my eyes and I'm grateful when Mac and Vito start in the direction of the kitchen, because I need some fucking coffee.

The guys let me make some coffee and sit at the island, inhaling a few sips before we continue talking about this. It has to relate somehow or there's no reason that they would've woke me up in the middle the night.

Mac leans against the counter next to the fridge, a ways from me. He's keeping tabs of everything. He's guarding us while we're talking. Always a soldier.

"One of the housekeeping staff called me a couple hours ago." Vito can see the confusion on my face. "Delano's housekeeping staff. Apparently Luca decided to end his parents last night and take over their rein."

"No shit," I say staring straight ahead, my thoughts occupying every second of my mind. I feel no sympathy for those people whatsoever, and I doubt if anybody else does, either. *They deserve it.*

I snap my head up to Vito and Mac. "What does this have to do with Avery and us?"

Vito sits down next to me. His skin is slightly pale, grayish looking. Dammit, this guy needs to go lay back down, but I know he won't, there's still too much to be taken care of.

"The housekeeper's staying with us right now. She's scared for her life since she came and told us everything that happened."

I can understand the asylum, but what is she so scared of? "What happened?"

"Luca killed both of his parents. He told everybody they could leave if they wanted to, or they could stay, but they have to remain loyal." Vito smirks at me before he continues. "Only eight people stayed."

I start to laugh, not a full-blown belly laugh, but enough that it's entertaining and amuses me right now. "I mean, I guess he should be happy that he got eight, he's a piece of shit."

"Apparently him and his new found men did not check the house thoroughly before they started talking about what they were going to do." Vito runs a hand through his hair looking a little bit disturbed. Even Mac looks like he's having trouble adjusting to all of this.

"Luca has three targets: me, you and Avery." My fists clench as my coffee cup lands hard on the island.

I know that Luca's always had trouble with Avery. I figured he wanted her more now since she's going to be the heir of the Romano Empire, but hearing there's a hit on her... I'm having trouble dealing with that. No motherfucker in this world is going to put a hit on my girl and live to tell about it, nobody. Even if it's his own personal hit. No one threatens Avery and lives.

"She couldn't hear all of the details, but she was able to get a few. She wasn't sure but she thinks that she heard gas or something to put everybody to sleep. She knew if she was caught she'd end up dead, so she escaped and came straight to us. And that's why we're waking you up."

I look between both men. "Have you guys interrogated her?" It's not really something that we like to do that much, but who knows if she's a plant sent here by Luca in the first place.

Vito shakes his head back and forth and so does Mac. "There's some you have to interrogate and there's some you don't, this one we don't. She's barely making it right now, the girl was absolutely terrified." Vito takes a breath, the man should be in bed. "She's pissed herself twice and we haven't even given her anything to drink. We've even had to stop her from talking a couple times because when we ask a question, she just word vomits every fucking thing. Even stuff that has nothing to do with any of this," Vito says as amusement sparks in his eyes. He can't get any better witnesses, except for the ones that have photographic memories.

I look at Vito, I expected him to be a little more pissed off, but he's not. Maybe he's relieved. We've talked so much and we've got over a lot of things that we want done in planning for Avery, what's best for her. One of the things that Vito was adamant about, was ending the whole Delano line. It looks like Luca just saved them a shit ton of time and energy. I just hope he's not upset he didn't get to do it himself. Those were the people that called for the deaths of his daughter, son-in-law and granddaughter.

"Let's reconvene in a few hours, maybe late morning. We can figure out what the hell we're going to do about the situation." Vito looks over to Mac. "Give the girl a couple tranquilizers, so that she can actually sleep. I bet you she's been up for over twenty-four hours. Her health will deteriorate if she doesn't relax soon."

Well shit, I'm on my second cup of coffee now, and I'm feeling pretty awake. I nod my goodbyes to the guys as I grab my cup and slowly work my way back to Avery.

After I shut the door and take a look at my girl, a devious thought goes through my head. We have a few hours anyway, *why not play*.

Avery is sleeping curled on her side with the blanket barely covering half of her body. I can make out the milky smooth skin of her back in the moonlight as I slowly strip away my clothes.

I don't know why I feel almost a sense of urgency

right now with her, maybe because I know that things are going to come to a head very soon.

When I crawl in bed next to her, I'm grateful that I don't have to figure out how to take off her clothes before slipping inside. She's still naked from last night.

I gently start to kiss and nibble at her back while my hands brush up and down her legs on the inside of her thighs and out. She starts to moan slightly and move. Maybe it's because of the coffee or everything that's happened but I really just want to yank her up and throw her against the wall and pound into her. My dick jumps at that thought, making me realize he's on board, too.

Avery starts to move around, slowly opening her eyes looking at me, "Asher?"

"Lay on your stomach, baby," I say as I maneuver her over. She gives me a big smile and practically jumps on her stomach making the whole bed shake. My girl is such a slut.

Avery slightly bend her knees giving me the perfect viewing position. I don't take long before I'm right at her back lining myself up and pounding myself into her.

She muffles her screams by stuffing her face into the pillow.

"Oh fuck," I snarl as I can't stop pounding. I'm relentless in my endeavors.

Less than two minutes in, Avery starts to scream, "Asher!"

Her body starts to clench around me, not releasing my dick, milking the bastard dry. I let the trembling slow down before I plop back on my back grabbing my girl to my side.

Nobody's ever gripped me that hard. My girl can make me come in an instant without even trying. It's like her body needs me to live, she just sucks and cleans me out every single time. I fucking love it.

Now, if only we can snooze for another hour or two.

"VITO WANTS US TO MEET HIM IN THE KITCHEN." I glance over at Avery, she's still messing around on her phone. Neither one of us were able to go back to sleep, even though we're both exhausted.

And shockingly enough after our third time, we both decided to get dressed. If I could be inside Avery all day, I would. Sometimes a man needs to eat and use the fucking bathroom. I never met another woman that can go as long as my girl, *thank God*.

"Are you ready?" Avery asks me as she holds out her hand waiting by the bedroom door. I grab her hand to my side as we both walk awkwardly down to the kitchen to meet with Vito.

I know exactly what he's showing us, and I respect that fact so damn much. Vito Romano is an awesome man, and from our many talks, I know that he respects me, hopefully just as much as I respect him.

He's helped with multiple situations in my own family business, he's like the father figure that I've never had. Shit, even the grandfather figure that I never had. I'll take him over any of my own family, definitely.

Vito smiles as he sees Avery walking into the room. She removes herself from me and wraps herself around Vito. At first I thought he might be annoyed every time that girl sees him now, she's always grabbing his hand and hugging and kissing him. Making up for lost time is what she told me once. Vito said he's missed out on this for so many years, and if she wants to hug him every second, then so be it.

We follow Vito until we're down in the basement in a makeshift gaming room that the guys and I threw up pretty fast. We're guys, we needed something to do, don't blame us.

Avery starts looking around awkwardly and then glances in Vito's direction. "Ping-pong tournament today?" We all chuckle, she's at least trying to break the ice. I know she hates not knowing what's going on. I can understand Vito not wanting to announce it.

He told me about this area, but I have yet to actually see it. Even Mac and the other guys don't know that it's here, only Vito and now us.

He grabs Avery's hand. "When you and Tate were searching for anything that you shouldn't find, you guys just didn't look hard enough." He heads into the closet off the bar that's been there since we got here.

We both watch with wonder, instead of turning the light switch on, Vito grabs it and turns it to the side, revealing the hidden open door in the back of the closet.

"Oh my God!" Avery shrieks as she runs toward the hidden area.

Yeah, Tate and Avery were pretty excited to go snooping yesterday, I can only imagine how much screaming they would've done if they would have found this.

The room isn't much to boast about. There's no hidden treasures and gold crowns littering the opening.

There's a huge safe in there, like one of those styles that you would see when you walk into a bank vault, not the big ones, but the ones in small towns that they leave in the corner. Boxes litter the edges of the walls, stacked up to three high.

I know Avery doesn't notice it, but I tear up just seeing the sadness and the love in Vito's eyes as he's watching his granddaughter gasp and run all over looking at the different things in here.

One day I'll tell her that, but for now I just want to remain invisible and let those two have their moment.

I wait outside the doorway where I can still hear what they're saying and make sure that everything's okay. It sucks now, though, because it just gives me time to think and remember the long talks I've had with Vito and how much he loves his granddaughter, and how much he respects me. I shake that thought away as I hear Avery laughing and squealing.

"Now, there's five-hundred grand in the safe. Some other families keep a larger amount of money, but all it takes is one break-in. Also, do not let anybody know what's down here besides just you and Asher, not even Tate or even Mac. I trust those two with my life, but slip-ups can always be made. You never want to say the wrong thing to the wrong person."

Vito angles his head toward the boxes lining the walls. "This is everything that I've amassed and gathered against the different families. Their most personal secrets, their enemies, even their extended family and immediate family. Anything that can give you a heads up if you ever need it." He gives Avery a hard look before he continues. "Don't be afraid to use something that they don't want to get out, if it's going to be the difference between life and death. Use it for whatever you need. Some of it might seem kind of shady but if this saves your life, it's definitely worth it."

I totally agree with Vito. Avery's got a good heart and soul but she needs to use everything to her advantage, especially in the world we live in.

She glances between the boxes and Vito. "Why not just put them all on a computer? A hard drive, then you don't have everything just sitting there. If a fire or something happened, you would lose it all."

Vito smiles, I know he's ingrained in his old ways just like a lot of the other bosses. "This would be something for the new boss to take care of. But I would recommend to not get rid of these, there's a lot of notes, info and age in these documents. The original seems to scare the shit out of people more than the technical version."

I glance at Avery, she's nodding her head up and down in total agreement with Vito. That makes me realize that mine is slightly nodding up and down, too, which also makes me chuckle, causing those two to stare at me.

"In the safe you'll find other shit like gold bars. Stocks and bonds. Deeds to all the different properties that we own. When I pass away..." Vito looks sternly at Avery saying this with as much determination as he can. I know he hates to talk about this, because it seems to crush her every time. "Let the lawyers and everyone else take care of this. I'll have Mac get you a folder of cards and shit of my trusted people." He looks around the room again. "I think I'll put the folder in here to make sure it's safe. The lawyers will handle everything, you won't have to worry about anything and all the properties will be transferred to your name." Avery's mood is turning somber now.

This talk has to happen, she needs to understand, and she needs to come to terms and deal with it. I give a nod to Vito, letting him know that I'll help in case she's not able to. He gives me a slight nod of his head back as a thank you. Man, this shit is fucking depressing.

"We have many accounts offshore. Business and personal accounts. Any kind of account you can think of, they probably have one of them set up." Vito wraps his arm around Avery. "Make sure you always have your money spread everywhere. I like to do at least fifty to one-hundred different accounts, even if you don't have that much money in each of them. They can't freeze all of your accounts when you have multiple ones in different countries. If you know something's coming down, you have a chance to pull at least some cash out. Only if you need more than what's in the safe to keep the businesses running. The IRS is the bigger bitch of an obstacle you will face over all of the other agencies. So watch your back with them and make sure that you're up-to-date."

Avery keeps nodding with wide eyes. She's been talking about going to business school and this is a lot of the shit that she has to learn. Vito lays out the account stuff right now, this will hurt, but I understand what he's saying. I'll do whatever I can to help her with that later.

We start to work our way back up to the kitchen after securing the area downstairs and making sure that no one followed us. Vito told all the men that the basement was off limits today, he just wants to be prepared.

"I don't want to move again," Avery says on a sigh

standing between both Vito and I holding onto both of our hands. We told her about the maid that was brought in.

"Then we're not going to," Vito says as he looks at Avery, then glances in my direction. I give him a nod in total agreement. "This is our house and we're not moving anymore. We'll just have to be stronger, faster and deadlier. So much fucking smarter than Luca."

Vito and Avery can see my grim expression and they understand me. We worked too hard and we fought too hard to run every time that little bitch comes around.

"There's no fucking way in hell we're moving again," I say as both Vito and Avery smile. We walk our happy asses upstairs because nobody's going to bring us down anymore, not even the Delano's.

CHAPTER 14

LUCA

We're stationed about two miles from the Romano compound. The seven guards and I are all dressed in black. We've even hid our faces in dark face paint. The kind that hunters use when they're trying to camouflage themselves out in the forest.

I'm more than certain it just makes us look like bigger idiots, but at least this way we can try to blend in a little. If this saves us from being caught, then it's fucking worth it. The guys actually do blend in. All of us have a light brown and green mix painting our faces.

All eight of us jump and aim our guns at the shuffling that we're hearing right at the clearing that we came into. Seth seems to drag a very frightened looking older gentleman still in his fucking lab coat closer to us.

"Were you able to get the agent?" I ask as I look between Seth and the guy.

"Sure did boss, but I figured I better bring him along to make sure that we administer it right, and we all don't knock ourselves on our asses."

The man has to be in his sixties with a graying receding hairline and very taut skin. He's shaking worse than anyone I've ever seen. And if his fear doesn't give him away, the wet crotch will work or the trickling of liquid leaking down right by his older style tennis shoes.

This guy is a chemical engineer, and my dog dresses better than him. I chuckle to myself. I don't have a dog but if I did he would dress better than this fucking idiot.

"Let's go," I say, as all of us start to walk. The man doesn't stop whimpering and crying and trying to explain to us how we could end up killing everybody, this is not a toy, blah, blah, blah.

"Shut him up," I snap at Seth who obliges me immediately. The sound of duct tape being ripped shows me exactly how he is going to shut him up.

The two-mile walk takes almost an hour. We can't come any closer because the rumbling of engines would definitely give us away. From our last recon we learned that Vito has well over three-hundred men camped at this estate right now. From my understanding, there's five-hundred acres besides the several buildings that sit on the land. The Mancini's had a ton more at their compound.

When Seth was torturing the engineer earlier, he said we just need to have a place to insert the liquid. It's only a few drops, but apparently it's enough to bring down the whole house. The heating system or the air conditioning system will work. Luckily for us, the AC is located on the outside of the house.

When we get there, the man starts rambling and fidgeting, clearly shaken about what he's about to do. "Multiple people could die, it doesn't mean that they'll be knocked out. There's a reason that this medicine isn't used that much." I'm on my last fucking nerve. I don't give a shit about the medicine. I don't even know the fucking name of the medicine. I pull out my gun and cock it, making sure the bite of the metal is indented in his temple. At this point in time I'm almost ready to pull the trigger but I need him to shut the fuck up and start working. If everyone dies in the house, so-fucking-be-it. I'd prefer it that way, but I want things done right, so I'll do it myself. Plus, I've been wanting to put my own bullets in the heads of Asher Mancini and Vito Romano.

He doesn't think longer than a second as he puts on a mask and gloves and pulls out a small vile from a little cooler that one of the guards had been carrying for him.

The only one that pays attention is Seth, while the rest of us make a tight circle formation. It's more like a crescent moon. We keep hidden, bending down. Thankfully Seth ripped off the white lab coat and the guy is wearing a lighter gray but he doesn't stick out like a moth to a flame now.

He lightly taps what can be no more than like ten drops into the air conditioning system. I figured he would just dump it on top into the fan, but he opens the system and puts it inside. I heard Seth say if he did it outside it can affect us just as much and we'd be on our ass. Fucking dumb ass, that's what he should've done. The engineer is never walking out of here, that's for damn sure, he knows too much.

The man takes in multiple breaths, they're shaky and most likely from fear. It could be the medicine affecting him. "In about twenty minutes, you should be ready." Perfect, I smile to myself and nod to Seth.

All of us are equipped with silencers, which merely makes a little clicking noise like a gush of air, a tiny boom, if you will.

The chemical engineer didn't even know what hit him, as he awkwardly falls to the ground. The guards move him behind the air conditioning unit. I personally don't give a shit if he stays right here, but when they start walking their rounds again, this scene is going to be a big red flag.

We might be able to knock out all the people inside, but we sure as shit can't knock out the fifty men out here. There's a total of nine of us with my seven guards, Seth and myself. I'm not in the mood to try to figure out how to fight six different men with automatic weapons and extensive training. I'm very well trained, so are the older guards, but I'm not sure if these younger dip shits in our group have been. My dad was a fucking deadly bastard, so they probably have been.

All of us return to our formations, but this time we lay on our stomachs, making sure that the whole area is clear. I have us wait for twenty minutes before we even move inside. Everyone out here waits in silence. Breathing is low and monitored. No noise is made, a sneeze or even gas. The guys better be sticking their face as far in the dirt as they can and squeeze those ass cheeks.

This is life and death, all of us know that. I'm either going to come out of here alive or dead. I'm going to come out of here either victorious or not victorious. As far as my men go, they are just the strength that is helping me move up in life, trying to get where I want to be, where I deserve to be. They're just hoping we make it. That I make it. Once I do have everything I want, I'm going to be the biggest mother fucker on the East Coast and maybe even after a while, I can start maneuvering and take over the West Coast, why the fuck not. I have the knowledge and the guys, I'll be fine.

I glance down at my watch and see that it's right on the dot at twenty minutes. I turn my head and nod to my guy on the right and he nods to the guy on his right, then I nod to the guy on my left, he does the same.

From the sounds of it, we could go in loud doing whatever the fuck we want, nobody would hear us, because they're out fucking cold, and it is in the middle the night. But there's always those little surprises. This medicine will affect others differently. There's a good chance that quite a few people will die and there is also a good chance that it might not hardly affect anyone at all, and they could still be awake, maybe sluggish.

We have to keep our shit together, every time we turn the corner, we never know what the fuck is going to be there.

Putting our gas masks on, we ease our way in through one of the open windows in the back laundry area. Luckily for us, it was right by the air conditioning units. Our luck is through the roof. I've heard stories of the security systems Vito has in place, and for one of the staff to leave the window cracked was a bad and deadly decision.

We're divided up into two teams. Seth, the older guards and I are on one team and the rest of them are on the other.

This is the best way for us to divide and conquer without risk of loss to everybody. Four or five guys in a fight is better than two, as we originally thought about doing five teams.

I nod to a door slightly ajar as we pass by. From what the blueprints told us, this is Romano's office.

Seth gets the message instantly and eases himself in there, not wanting to even try to push the door open, afraid that it might creak. The rest of us start searching rooms, this is a big house but I did not think that there would be this many unoccupied fucking bedrooms. I know that the guards have locations off of the campus to sleep but from my understanding, Vito's having them around the house at all times, because of me.

I enter a room, which looks to be the master bedroom. It's larger than all the other rooms that we have been in. I spot a single form sleeping on the bed. I make my way over there, silently, because who knows if the chemicals actually worked. I always heard Vito sleeps with one fucking eye open. He isn't even acknowledging us right now. The only reason I recognize the prick is because of that family fucking ring he's got on his finger. I yank it off to see if he moves. He doesn't, I easily slip the Romano crest onto my finger.

Even though I have a silencer, I still want to remain as invisible and unnoticed as possible. I quickly drag the pillow out from underneath Vito's head, hoping that he'll just wake up for an instant, but he doesn't. I slam the pillow on his face and pull the trigger three times.

Excessive, yes. But I need to make sure that motherfucker is dead.

Two more targets and then we are out of here. I nod to one of my guys at the doorway and they continue on down the hall, searching. I thought this would be easy for me as I make my way out the door, but I honestly don't know if I could do what I just did to Vito to Avery. I might need to have Seth do it, but I want to be first in line for when they get Asher.

We spend the next thirty minutes searching the house completely. For the life of us, we cannot find Avery or Asher anywhere. There's no way that they could've known we were coming or what we planned on doing. We told no one.

Shots start going off on the other side of the house, snapping all of our attention in that direction. "Go, go, go!" I scream to my guys. Seth and I hang back as we continue to move forward. I'm being extra cautious right now, if there's people that are awake, who knows if the chemicals even worked effectively like they were supposed to.

"Fuck," I hiss as quietly as I can to myself. I really want to scream at the top of my fucking lungs.

There's movement on the other side of the hallway as I alert Seth in that direction. There is no way we could be seen over here. Besides the soft moonlight that's coming in, we're both covered in darkness. All of us are. But that doesn't stop whoever's at the end from noticing movement or maybe a reflection.

They point and it takes me a second to realize that it's Avery and Asher. Both Seth and I pull out our guns and start firing.

I start to crawl against the wall, keeping my head

down but my eyes up. It'll be harder to hit me and see where I'm at. I keep popping off shots.

Asher screams, the rumble feels like it enters and shakes my bones. I swear the house even shifted. "Run, Avery!" Avery doesn't take a second to adjust to the scream that tortured our souls.

I chuckle, this is kind of fun. As soon as we both make eye contact, Avery can tell it's me. She screeches and then takes off down the hallway.

I smile big, I love the game of cat and mouse. I didn't think it was going to go like this, it's going to be one hell of a night.

CHAPTER 15

AVERY

"Come with me, I want to show you something." Asher grabs my hand and slightly tugs. We had just left the secret room that Vito showed us in the basement.

"Okay." It's not like I have anything else better to do right now. Vito said he was feeling a little tired, so he went and laid down.

Asher leads us to the attic. "Come on, it's not that far." I'm glad he said something because this place is freaking me the fuck out. There is a reason that Tate and I avoided the attic and that's because it hasn't been touched in probably at least one-hundred years. I know there are spiders in here, at least as big as my hand. Asher chuckles slightly when I curl my body around his.

The attic is huge, it covers the whole expanse of the cabin. When we get further, it's not as dusty as I thought it would be, but it's still really dirty. I think the thing that shocked me the most is there's not that much stuff up here. There's the normal boxes and baby items, probably from my mother, but that's it.

I pass by a box and run my finger over it, looking at the inch of dirt that came off. All the attics I've seen on TV shows, even reality shows, are just cluttered to the brim. This is the area that everybody puts the shit that they don't want anymore, but are too lazy to get rid of.

"We're almost there, come on." Asher is excited to show me whatever he has planned. So I smile big, his happiness seeping through me.

Behind several boxes and an old chair is a door. Now I'm more intrigued to snoop. Curiosity is seeping through my pores, wondering where this goes. I can't wait to tell Tate what I found, or what Asher showed me, she's going to be just as pissed that we didn't go into the attic.

The door opens and Asher makes his way through, leaving me trailing close behind. "Oh my God," I say as we practically open the door to the roof.

It's not the roof that I'm interested in, no. The Romano's have changed this into a freaking atrium, glass is everywhere and it's absolutely beautiful.

Asher comes close to me and wraps his arm around me from behind, my back fits snugly against his chest. "Vito was exhausted but he wanted you to see this place." We continue to walk, but this time he comes around to my side and holds my hand as we explore.

"This was all your grandmothers doing, but she passed before she was really able to enjoy it."

In my head, I feel like crying, thinking about her, but I don't want to miss anything. I blink the tears away repeatedly. No one's been in here for at least ten or fifteen years.

Even the attic looks cleaner than the atrium does.

I gasp as my hand goes over my mouth when I look in the corner part of the atrium. This is absolutely stunning. I have a view of everything around, except for my back where the wall is. Stars are shining so bright.

"You brought a bed up?" I ask as I look at Asher and he smiles knowingly. He knows that I would love this.

I squeal with delight, throwing my arms around him. "This is awesome." I look around some more, seeing the candles and bottle of chilled wine, with wine glasses next to it. "Does this mean that we get to sleep out here tonight?" Asher is nodding. "I want to make this our new bedroom."

Asher shakes his head no. "There is no running water or electricity out here. In the winter I imagine it's really damn cold, even though it's enclosed in glass."

The door that leads onto the roof slightly opens and out comes a grumpy Sneaker. I release Asher's hand and snuggle up to the old asshole.

Wow, there's so much light in here during the day, I bet the stars are so bright at night. This is a perfect area for a garden, and looking around I can tell that's what my grandma intended to use it for. It's magical.

There are multiple dust covered flower boxes everywhere. I wonder if she ever got to try it for at least one year to see how pretty it was and if it worked. I need to ask Vito about that, I doubt if Asher knows.

Asher engulfs me in a hug again. "With everything going on I feel much safer if we're out here tonight than inside." Shit, maybe we should ask Vito, Mac, and Tate if they want to come, I think to myself.

"I mentioned it to everybody else and they want us just to have our time tonight," Asher answers, knowing what I'm thinking.

"You are too perfect." I wrap my arms around him, letting him know just how much I appreciate him.

"Stop," I mumble out, swatting at whatever's trying to wake me up. Something keeps tickling my face and licking me.

My eyes open and I stare into the grumpy face of Sneaker. I look over at the door and it's slightly ajar, we must've not closed it all the way last night. I go to pet the ass, but before I reach him, he falls right over.

Sitting up quickly, I grab Sneaker in my hands, normally the little shit always likes to hiss at me, but not this time. "What's wrong buddy?"

I set him down on his feet and just watch him

constantly running into anything that's within ten feet of him. He seems to angle over to it. He hit a few flower pots and even ran into the wall.

This is not good, something's up inside the house for Sneaker to be acting like this.

"Asher," I put my hand on his shoulder and push trying to wake him up. He normally sleeps with one eye open but is like dead to the world. "Asher, get up now." I start pushing harder on him.

He opens his eyes rubbing them to get them to clear up. "What's going on?" He looks at me and then looks around, finally landing on Sneaker. I don't say anything as he just watches the old cat trip and fall over himself multiple times.

Asher starts to chuckle before he gets a look at my expression and quickly zips his mouth shut. If this was any other situation, like if he had to have surgery or something, it'd be freaking hilarious, especially with this old ass hole, but I feel down deep in my bones that something is wrong.

Asher glances at the doorway and then back at the cat and then starts looking around at the area we're sleeping in. He has come to the same conclusion I have, but ten times faster.

He nods at me. "Let's go." He doesn't have to tell me twice. Both of us jump up and get dressed in less time than it took to take off our clothes.

Both of us head over to the door as quietly as we can. Asher puts his finger up to his mouth when he starts to pull the door open more. I nod, I sure as shit don't feel like talking now.

I glance back over at Sneaker, who has already decided our bed is the best place for him right now. The old shit's already snoring, peacefully asleep. Hopefully he'll feel better and gets whatever's in his system out.

Asher lifts the collar of my shirt and places it over my face. He's doing his the same way in case there's any fumes or gas in the air.

Both of us slowly sneak down, not making any iota of noise. It could just be something stupid, but the lives we live, I doubt that's possible. Something bad is going down.

Two floors down and we're back on the first level. Both of us are starting to feel a little relaxed because we haven't noticed anything. That's when the hairs on my body, the tiny little ones that never come out, are fully engulfed and standing straight up. My mom always taught me to pay attention to those hairs, they'll let you know when something is wrong. Asher is the same way, none of us let our guard down even though we both want to relax. I would love to run to Tate's and my grandpa's room and make sure they're okay. If this gas is doing that much to Sneaker, I can only imagine what it's doing to them. He's smaller I guess, but he got outside right away.

Pop, pop, pop. Shots are fired, startling the crap out

of Asher and me. We both jump what feels like ten feet into the air.

We lean against the wall as fast as we can. "It sounds like they're coming from outside," Asher whispers in my ear.

He reaches behind his back and pulls out a gun. I didn't even think to check for weapons or grab something as we were coming down, but I doubt if I can do much damage with the garden hose.

I nudge Asher when I see something reflective down at the end of the hall. We both freeze and he positions himself in front of me as much as he can.

It looks like two figures. I can barely make out any attributes on them. They must be covered in all black. The more I stare, it seems the more my eyes can adjust to the darkness. I gasp slightly and then whisper out, "Luca."

He must hear me at the same time as Asher. That's when the guns they have aimed our way start popping off. Both Asher and I get down, as he starts firing back toward them.

"Run, Avery!" Asher yells as loud as he can. The gunshots are loud but not too loud.

I'm unarmed and I know that they're probably here for me, so it's better to make my way away from everybody. I don't want to leave Asher's side, but at this point in time if I don't, I put us both in danger.

I look for the closest means of escape, which is

another hallway, thankfully this one leads to Tate's room and the other guys.

"Asher, you should just give me the girl and I promise to let all of you walk out of here." I couldn't hear what Asher said back to him. I'm pretty sure he told him to fuck off.

I don't think I can get my body any closer to the wall than I am now. My clothes are darker but not the color of darkness, so I'm not as invisible as I would like. I keep my back plastered against the wall, ignoring the bite of pain from the texture pinching and digging into my skin.

I breathe a sigh of relief and say a quiet thank you as I find Tate's door and shut myself inside. It's a bitch to keep my face covered. And the only reason I could tell it was Luca before is from the color of his eyes. Plus, what other fucking idiot would be in this house in the middle of the night.

There's three-hundred guards. That makes my breath almost escape, leaving me winded. Where are the three-hundred guards now? And why does this house seem so eerily deserted?

"Tate, wake up." I keep pushing on my friend trying to get her to wake up. I even smack her a couple times in the face, not hard. Most people that are being smacked in the face will wake up extremely pissed. Not Tate.

There's something in the ventilation system, there's gotta be. I spot a few bandanas on the nightstand over by Tate's dresser. When she doesn't feel like doing her hair, she just wraps it in a bandana from the back, like a southern girl.

I wrap one around my face and then wrap one around Tate's. My best friend is tiny, but weighs a ton when it's deadweight. I swear it takes me at least half an hour, but it was probably only five minutes, to move her.

There's a little loveseat over by the window in the corner of the room. I moved the loveseat out a little bit and stuffed my friend back there. Opening the window as far as I can, I check to make sure her mouth is covered. Hopefully she'll be able to wake up soon and won't have as many ill effects from this fucking drug.

I just wish I had the energy to drag her around with me. I'll come back and check up on her soon.

I look back and forth in a panic. I have no idea what the fuck I'm supposed to do now. I don't think it's safe for me to stay and hide with Tate in this room. Besides the closet, there's no other place for me to go. The bed is totally open underneath. It's one of those log cabin style beds you can see everything. I won't be able to hide under there, either.

I put my back against the wall next to the door. "I can do this," I whisper to myself. There's no time like the present.

I take a deep breath to see if my little pep talk worked, it didn't but I have no choice. I open the door, sneaking into the hallway looking both ways. I should probably get down in an army crawl, but if I need to run that's gonna really fuck me up.

A sob wants to break out as I look into the darkness. The men that are in this house right now are here for only one reason and that's to get rid of us, nothing else. If I'm not smart about this, I'm done.

I look back out into the hallway and decide to go down to the guards' room. It's farther down but at least maybe I could see if they're okay. Who knows, some of the guys could be awake.

We have more guards' quarters on the property, but we also like to keep some in the house in case there's an emergency. This is one of the nicer suites up here. In the basement by the gaming room there's a bunch of other ones. The one up here can only sleep six or seven. I believe there were three bunk beds and one queen-size bed.

I count the doors as I try to control my breathing and my shaking. I inch my way down as slowly as I can, not making any noise. I'm lucky that nobody is in this hallway right now. I don't hear any shooting, shouting, or guns firing.

As soon as I reach the door, I yank it open and run inside. On instinct my hand goes to slam it but I grab it with my other one and slightly close it.

Half of the bunk beds are full with guys that are out. I cover my mouth and the gasp that comes out when I notice the queen bed on the side of the room has Mac in it. He's out cold, just as bad as Tate was. I don't have enough handkerchiefs for everybody, so I place the one I have left on Mac and open the windows in the room hoping that helps everybody. I don't know if it will. What's knocking everyone out must be coming in through the vents, that's the only way that it could be.

I've been in this house long enough that I'm starting to feel a little lightheaded.

I need to make my way outside or I'll end up passing out like the rest of them and then for sure I'll be dead when they find me.

It doesn't take much to kick out the screen in Mac's window. Fuck, I think it'd be awesome if there was a security system panel here. I know we have one of the best but they're not in this room. It should be in this room, this is where some of the guards sleep that need to have access and control to it.

This is something I need to tell Vito later.

I'm not even trying to be graceful, but I'm trying to be quiet. There's no way that I'll be able to be both. I dive headfirst out of the window. Luckily I'm still young and I can remember my tumbling days so I don't snap my neck by landing headfirst into the grass below the window.

I stand with my back toward the window, I angle myself and grab what looks to be a little flashlight off the nightstand next to Mac.

I can see many guards hundreds of yards away just patrolling the area. I don't know the SOS signal, so I just start flashing the light their way, hopefully they'll see and start running back to help.

After five minutes I'm able to get a few of their attention and half of the men start running back in this direction. I sag against the pinewood of the house, taking deep breaths and just praying to God that everybody comes out of this okay, except for Luca. I hope they shoot that bitch right before killing whoever he brought with him.

Now it's just a vile waiting game, hopefully we just come out on top.

CHAPTER 16

Asher

The smell of gunshots and copper is overwhelming. I know I've got to get out of this house and soon. If I can smell all the other shit, then whatever has knocked everybody else out is going to end up doing the same to me. If that happens then I consider all of us dead. There's no way I'm gonna let anybody take Avery from me.

I'm hiding in a small enclave on the first floor, not far from where we originally came down. *Luca*, I have no idea how Avery can tell it's him, but she knows for sure, and what has to be his right-hand man, Seth, are the ones down at the end of the hall. My eyes have adjusted and now I can make out the two figures and see what they're doing, see their movements. Their outfits did help, but that was more for surprise. When you're in complete darkness, it takes a while until your eyes are back to normal.

Where the fuck is everybody? There's no way in hell that everyone would've been knocked out. Unless it's circulating through the air, right at that time is when the air conditioner decides to click on again. I can't smell anything over the gunshots. Everything smells like copper and metal. That's gotta be where it's coming in. At least now I have a freaking plan.

My gun is in my hand and a couple of clips are securely tucked in my pocket. Thankfully I remembered to grab them when we were coming down from the atrium. I need a better advantage so I can see those guys a little more. I'm not worried about getting rid of both Luca and Seth, but I don't know if there's anybody else way down at the end of the hall. Hopefully they just thought I up and left with Avery, because they haven't been firing anymore, just looking in my direction.

I decide not to take a chance and army crawl. I need to make it somewhere I can slip out. I need to get outside to that air conditioning unit and shut it off. That makes me think of where the actual control is at. If I can shut it off from inside, I wouldn't have to go through all that other shit.

Dammit, I don't know where the controls are, but I did see air-conditioners outside. I can fuck those up at least, then whatever's coming in won't be coming in anymore.

This will only work if that's the cause. One of the housekeeping staff could've just dropped something in our dinner or put something in our drinks, I doubt it though. Our staff is too loyal and paid too well to ever turn. Besides, they know what will happen to them and their families.

I'm disoriented after a couple minutes. I know I'm breathing in too much, I try to wrap my shirt around my face, but that doesn't work very well.

"Fuck it," I say as I yank the whole shirt off. It's a darker color so it was helping to keep me hidden. I wrap the whole thing layered around my mouth and nose.

I stand up as soon as I'm out of view from Seth and Luca. I have no idea what those two are doing, but their focus is intently on each other.

Luckily for me, I'm by the laundry and kitchen area which has a convenient little back door. The power's off, at least in here it is. I did briefly think about activating the alarm that's located by the door I want to exit through.

It's in our best interest to call the police, but then it's also not. The guards won't call and neither will any of the staff. It will come down to me, Vito or Avery who decides to call. I'm pretty sure Avery's not even thinking it is an option.

In the world that we grew up in, no matter what happens, you never call. If somebody wrongs you then your whole damn family will make it right. It goes the same way if you wrong somebody else, they'll make it right. The families decide to fix their own problems, delivering justice that they see fit, definitely not in the eyes of the law.

I have some handyman skills, but I would rather deal with guns and knives and other shit. My handyman skills vary just from basically watching TV and being asked to help with something by Avery or one of the other guys.

The blades are turning in the air conditioning units. There's a long thick cord that angles directly back into the house. I can see lights in different sections of the house and the AC units are working, so they must've just disabled the alarm system and left everything else alone.

"Fuck!" I wish they would've shut everything off.

There ain't no way I'm going for that big cable and frying myself, possibly starting a huge fire. If everybody's knocked out inside, they're all going to burn alive, if they don't have a bullet in them.

I do the next best thing in the limited amount of time I have. There are some unused boards leaning against the side of the house for when we were helping to reconstruct the fence that's been down for years. In six months, we still haven't finished fencing in this huge estate.

There are three AC units and luckily there's several boards, so I have enough. I look around to make sure nobody's watching as I jab one of the boards right through the top easily breaking through the metal protection grate. I make sure my grip is good before I slam the post down in between the blades. It makes a grunting noise. I quickly do this to the other ones and then run away. Everything I've seen on TV, if you stop something like this it ends up blowing up and scattering shit everywhere. I know it's not going to be quiet and I don't care. This is the only option I have to get those things busted.

I run quickly back the way I came, shutting the door softly behind me. I need to find Avery and I need to find Vito. Thankfully my sense of direction is back as I press myself against the wall and slightly curl down making my way to Vito's room.

"Fuck," I say quietly as I tiptoe down to Vito's room. I was by the garage, I should've looked in there for more weapons.

There's an area on the side of the garage, it's basically locked storage. A lot of the guards keep their weapons here so they don't have to take them home with them. Only Mac and Vito know the codes, but luckily for me I've seen them use it.

For now I'm pushing forward, I need to get to Vito.

I put myself in a little corner of the wall when I can hear screaming followed by a couple shots popping off. The three men that run by covered in pure black don't even notice me, thank God.

I wait till they reach the end of the hallway and turn and then slip inside Vito's room.

Thankfully it's not locked, and he's not waiting with a gun at my head.

"No," I gasp as a single tear runs down my cheek. I pull the pillow back on Vito's head and see that they got to him first. "Fuck!" I can feel my heart clenching and breaking right in my chest. This man didn't deserve to go out like this. This is going to break Avery. These last few precious minutes with her grandfather were everything to her. She didn't have much time left and they took it, they cut it short.

All I want to do is scream and rage, but I've got to get my shit together. I take a deep breath and I start frantically searching Vito's room as quietly as I can. I'm glad I did that, I find another handgun, four clips and a knife.

The knife was under Vito's pillow. It looks like when they grabbed the pillow to kill him, they left it in plain view. How the idiots didn't see it, I have no clue.

Now it's time for all these fuckers to die before they get to Avery. There's no way in fucking hell I'm going to let that happen, not on my watch and definitely not while I'm alive.

The shirt around my face is blocking half of my vision, so I yank the thing off and then put it back on hoping that it will be a deterrent, or at least maybe somebody won't notice me. I got lucky about five minutes ago but that's because their attention was focused on something ahead.

I angle my way out of the room, silently telling Vito

goodbye and then shut the door behind me, my back is still pressed against the wall listening and figuring out where that son of a bitch is.

It doesn't take long till I can hear noise coming from my left toward the foyer and Vito's office.

It sounds like Luca's talking to one other person but I can't make out the words, I'm still too far.

"Where the fuck is she? Have you guys searched the whole house?" I move closer, but I can barely see them, it looks like Seth nods his head.

"She's got to be here somewhere, I can still see their cars, so she hasn't left yet. She's just hiding well. Get the remaining guys together, we need to take out Asher and Avery before all that shit wears off and everybody wakes up."

"Got it boss," Seth says on a whisper, but luckily for me I inch myself closer. I'm lining up the perfect shot. I don't have a silencer like everybody else has been using. The silencer has hurt us, because we cannot figure out where everybody's at. It was smart on their end to bring it, even though they planned on killing everybody anyway.

I would aim for Luca a thousand times over Seth, but the right-hand man is blocking his boss. I'm not waiting for a perfect chance again. I need to get this over with, both of them need to die.

I aim up my shot perfectly. The boom from the gun is deafening in the silence, making my ears ring. I glance up a second later and see that Seth has fallen. A big hole is right in the back of his head.

Luca is giving me a look right now that if it was possible in our world, I would be dead, if looks could kill.

I jump up from my hidden position and get ready to engage the bitch, both of us are aiming our guns at each other.

This is something I've been waiting for ever since I met Avery Mila Romano. The woman of my dreams, the woman I'm going to marry, this fucker needs to die, hopefully painfully.

"Asher." Both of us snap our heads in that direction. Avery is hidden behind a door but between the cracks I know that Luca can see her. My body is angled toward her now. I'm about to start yelling for her to run away when Luca gets off a shot.

Avery starts screaming as a bullet enters my upper left thigh and exits through the right side of my right thigh. That fucker double penetrated me. If we were friends, this would be an epic joke at lame parties.

I go straight down, I don't tip forwards, backwards, to any of the sides. No, I fall like a bag of fucking bricks, straight down right on to my ankles. I can hear the bones crack as I land. The pain is excruciating and unbearable.

Avery starts running to me, and Luca starts to laugh as he fires in her direction. I'm barely staying conscious. I know I'm losing a lot of blood. The fucker probably hit an artery. I need to get her out of here and make sure that she's safe before it's too late.

Another shot rings out and Avery jerks painfully to the side, sliding down the wall. "No!" I scream. I know I'm close to death, so my scream probably came out as a whisper yell.

The room is filling with darkness. I try to fight, scream, drag myself toward her. The pain and the darkness are calling for me to surrender. All I know is that if I go under, we're all as good as dead, but I can't help it. The pain is too strong. I have no choice, the light is getting sucked away from me by the second. I don't smell the metallic of guns or the coppery smell of blood anymore. I don't smell anything.

I can barely even see. I just want one last look at Avery, nothing ever works the way we want to as the darkness pulls me under.

CHAPTER 17

AVERY

The bullet that entered my shoulder slammed me against the wall. For a couple seconds I had the worst pain that I've ever experienced in my life. Unfortunately the blast from the gun knocked me hard into the wall and knocked my ass flat on the ground.

I was out cold.

It couldn't have been for very long, one of the guards starts kicking me. At least it wasn't a full debilitated kick that startled me awake, he was only checking for life.

You know when you first wake up in the morning, you just want to jump out of bed sometimes or open your eyes and yawn and stretch. I think the only thing that saved my life is that I didn't do either.

All I want to do is scream, the pain is relentless and maddening, I'm biting my tongue and doing everything

I can to stay in this position where the guard thinks I'm dead or almost there.

Thankfully after a few slightly painful kicks he stops and I can hear the static and clicking from his radio.

"All three are dead, let's get out of here," the guard says.

I don't know if he's just saying this for me, just to see if I am truly dead. Maybe they don't have any more bullets. But I remain unmoving, the excruciating pain that has torn through the meaty part of my body is also breaking my heart in two. The guard said three people and there were only three targets: me, Vito and Asher. Oh God, does that mean that they're all dead?

Calm down, I keep telling myself in my head. They think I'm dead, maybe the others are just playing possum or maybe they got the wrong people. Yeah, that could be it.

I'm still in hell, I can't move because I can feel him watching me. His eyes are staring holes through my body, making this unimaginable pain drag on.

The only thing that's keeping me from screaming and just doing everything and anything I can to bring these men down is the fact that they still might be alive.

If they are, are they in as much pain as I am? Maybe they're just knocked out.

The guard's footsteps walking away gets me out of my very unhealthy thought process. I can hear the static of the radio crackling again. "I checked the others, let's get out of here, we're done, Rob."

Oh God, I clamp my mouth shut as a sob tries to break free. That was Luca's voice on the radio. He checked the others to verify that they were dead.

The guard walks away leaving me in my own little pool of blood and despair.

Unfortunately for them, the rage is building stronger as it pumps through my veins, getting rid of all the pain and enticing my revenge.

I slowly crack open my right eye, just a slit at the bottom, in case that fucker is standing right there. I take in a deep breath and let it go when I notice the coast is clear.

I drag myself to the nearest bathroom. It starts as an army crawl that moves up to a crawl and then finally I find the strength to lift myself up, using the wall for leverage. I feel like dead weight, like I weigh double of what I did this morning.

I need to stop the blood from seeping out. Too much keeps coming out. I'm no doctor, but I don't think there's a huge artery in the arm or the shoulder that would cause me to lose this much blood.

I spot a nearby bathroom. It takes everything I have to get there. I'm running on reserves trying to clean some of the mess that is my arm.

The pain has morphed into madness, which helps me to do a somewhat sufficient sling around my arm in under two minutes.

As I get ready to open the door, more shots pop off. They sound a little farther away but one shot for me is enough, close or not. I drop to my knees and cover my head silently rocking back and forth. The anger is still there, but the emotional pain of seeing and hearing a gun again is working horrors on my psyche right now.

"I need to get out of here," I whisper to myself. I'm the only one that can avenge my family if it's true what the guard said about Asher and Vito.

I have to get out of here. *Now!*

I'm moving on adrenaline as I slowly creep the hallways biting my tongue not letting a painful whimper escape. There are men down everywhere, these must've been the guards that came from outside, mixed with Luca's men.

A horrible thought goes through my mind and of course it's something that Luca would do. Kill everybody while they're sleeping. That asshole probably didn't even bring that many guys.

Looking at the ground around me I can see bodies of men who do not work for us. I've only heard one guard still alive talking with Luca. He hardly brought anyone with him.

I start to move faster. My first thought was to stay alive but now my main goal is to not let Luca escape alive.

I make out a familiar figure lying about one-hundred feet in front of me. This isn't the same spot I left Asher, but it's close enough. I drop to my knees ignoring the sob that goes through me, the one that's been wanting to escape the pain and shit that we've been through in this life.

I touch his face and gasp, he's still really warm. "Asher," I whisper at him. "Please wake up, they're gone." Asher doesn't move.

I look down at my knees where I dropped down next to him and they're covered in his sticky blood. He has no wounds on the top part of his body, it's all lower.

Guards rush in, grabbing my attention making me push myself as far back against the wall as I can. Thankfully, and I'm thanking God for this a million times over, they're our guards.

They rush in and drop next Asher checking him over. One of them even has a first aid kit in their back pocket. They probably all do which is pretty smart. A sob escapes again as I think about talking to Vito about them carrying that. But I know deep in my heart that there is no more Vito. The guards glance in my direction, they never even noticed I was there.

"Avery, we've got to get you out of here." I nod. I don't want to be here right now.

Out of the corner of my eye I spot two men dipping and diving, so to speak, making their way to an SUV that's parked five-hundred yards away.

I look back at the guards about ready to say something, but there's only two of them in here and they both are needed to take care of Asher. I have to do this on my own.

I tighten my sling, making me bite my tongue hard drawing a little blood. I need my fucking arm to not fail me now. Hopefully the blood will slow down until I kill Luca.

I slip down the hallway past the guards. I probably don't need to hide what I'm doing, these are Vito's men. I guess they're my guards now, too. I wipe away the tears and shake my head. I'm not doing this shit now. I need to be fully concentrated on making sure this bitch burns.

From what I can make out, those two were heading toward a newer SUV not far away, so I don't have that much time. They're moving slowly not to draw attention to themselves, because there are still a shit ton of our guards outside. We do have an alarm system that can alert them in the house but there's no way I'm hitting it. Luca deserves to die, and I deserve to do it.

Once I'm in the clear, away from the guards, I start to run. You never realize how weak you are until you lose a shit ton of blood. Nothing's going to stop me, not even blood loss.

Once in the garage, I start sifting through tons of keys that are everywhere. This is a twelve car garage and there about ten different vehicles in here, from a beat up SUV to a freaking Bentley. I've never see my grandpa riding in a Bentley, maybe he just had it for show, or maybe my grandma wanted it. There are keys on the edge of the toolbox, I grab them and hit the fob letting me know who they belong to.

I smile as I take in the black Maserati. This would not be my choice, it'd be better for me to have the old crappy SUV but I have no idea where the keys are and my time is very limited.

I jerk my head up to see if I can see them anymore, but luckily for me they're just getting to the SUV now. I jump in the car, get everything ready, even opening another garage door on the backside so that they don't see me. I want them to get a little bit ahead. At least I think that if they believe they're safe, then they won't keep looking for anybody behind them.

Those two are not getting away, I want their heads on a fucking pike in our front yard.

Of course, we'll have to leave them inside the house, this isn't the medieval times.

I watch them, feeling the anger boiling in my veins as Luca and the guard are laughing and patting each other on the back. I have no idea how I'm able to see this well, especially in my weakened state. I've always had awesome eye sight, but this is ridiculous, maybe I'm just seeing what I want. I shake my head at that thought, I know that's not even true, Luca is acting exactly how Luca does, selfish and self-centered. That's why even if he gets away from us, he won't last long. Other families will tear him down, he's pretty much the epitome of fucked.

I start the Maserati and the thing bursts to life. I

need to show him that if you mess with the Romano's and the Mancini's, you won't walk away, and all of this delivered by a fucking woman.

I sound mad and crazy!

I pound the steering wheel as I slowly start to creep after them. It's time to get my revenge.

CHAPTER 18

AVERY

Waiting and just watching from the Maserati allows my anger to build. Every second that that coward and his guard, Bob, are not dead makes me want to set the world on fire. I don't even care right now if I have to watch the whole fucker burn.

Rage.

All I see is red, since I don't have the people that matter the most to me anymore, I don't even know if Tate or anyone is still alive. I want to tear down all of the Mancini and Romano enemies in one little area and watch them burn. Watch them scream.

The SUV is far enough away so I ease the Maserati out of the garage, not even bothering to shut the door behind me, who fucking cares. A thought goes through my head that makes me laugh. Robbers will think we're an easy target with the garage door open, but wait until they get a load of all the bodies.

When I start to drive a little faster, I realize I don't have a freaking plan at all. All I know is that I will do anything that it takes to get rid of these men, even if I die in a fiery blaze with them.

I glance up toward the sky and whisper, "I'm sorry." Sorry for the fact that I'm about to destroy this beautiful car, and sorry for the fact that I'll be visiting with you guys soon.

I chuckle, at least I couldn't find the keys to the fucking Bentley. I imagine the gates of hell would open then for me. I'm full on laughing and crying, I'm such an emotional fucking wreck right now.

I have no plan but the only thing I know is that I have a very small chance, maybe less than five percent, of actually walking or being carried out of here alive.

This car is my weapon and Luca and I are both dying today. To make sure of his death, I will go to the gates of hell with him. I will drag that fucker there, screaming and fighting myself if I have to.

It's still somewhat dark out so I flip off my lights. I almost thought about shutting off the dome lights, too, but I'm not exactly sure where the controls are. It's got to be around the light switch somewhere. I need to see something so I'm not just totally doing a shot in the dark here, hoping I don't end up in a ditch.

I do need to slow down now, driving in the dark is not easy. When my eyes adjust, it helps a little bit. I have tears, sweat and blood around my eyes. Everything burns, I'm just hoping I can stay on the fucking road.

I expected us to be driving for miles upon miles, what I didn't expect is for them to turn off in an area five miles down the road. Did they already find somebody else's house to steal? Or maybe they're going to try to do it now.

Yeah right, they are not going to harm another person in this life.

I'm about one-hundred feet behind now with no lights as they slowly turn in to the long driveway leading up to one of the nicer houses in this area.

There's no time like the fucking present. I scream as loud as I can at the same instant that I downshift and press the gas pedal all the way down to the floor.

This time I turn on the lights so that they can see what's coming. So they know that they're about to be rammed by another vehicle.

Whether I die or whether I live, I want Luca's shocked expression etched into my brain forever. He has his mouth wide open and his eyes are even bigger, as I race toward him. He's talking fast, but it looks like he's slowly mouthing words to his guard. Shifting to third gives me an extra boost right before I slam into the side of the SUV.

My car slams into them, jerking me back into my seat, causing my head to painfully bounce. Shockingly they start flipping. It's even better that they were next to a ditch for the excess rainwater that happens here in Chicago. They had to flip at least four or five times until they landed on their side.

The crack of metal crunches together, and the screams of the men can be heard, probably for miles. I look at the guard who took the brunt of the accident since he was driving.

I grab my gun that I found next to Asher and put it in my back pocket. I have a knife in my left hand. My right hand is open in case I need to use it. The knife in my left hand won't do any good since I have a hole through my shoulder but I can carry it, shockingly.

"Ouch," I say looking down to the guard who is looking at me with wide eyes but is unfortunately pinned by the total weight up to his chest from the SUV. "I bet you wish you would've worn your seatbelt now, huh?"

The lights from the Maserati are lighting up every-thing where I can get a glimpse of myself in one of the SUV's windows. I am covered in blood, basically from my head down to my toes. I got blood from different wounds and people. Some is from fighting earlier, being hit, and the wound on my arm won't stop bleeding.

I look like a fucking bad ass, *a dead one*. The wound must've opened up again.

At first I thought about ending it for the guard, but he's not going anywhere and even if he does, I bet you everything is broken and shattered inside of his body. His skin is starting to turn a gaudy gray color.

Luca grabs my attention. I can see he's desperately searching for some kind of weapon to use. His gun must've gotten lost in the wreckage. He's kind of an idiot, if he would've taken the seat belt off, he would've had more room to move around and find something.

"Avery, we can talk about this." He stumbles, searching for the right words. "Between the two of us, we can take over the whole fucking world, I can work for you."

I chuckle as I remove my gun with my good arm, my right arm.

"What are you doing?" Luca cries out.

I don't say anything, I just point the gun at his dick, trying to line up the best I can. Before I pull the trigger, I make sure to glance up and smile. I got hit in the head a few times, too, so the blood is going down my face, I'm pretty sure it's covering my teeth. Damn, I need to take a picture so I can actually see what I look like, the reflection is not doing me justice.

I laugh to myself, my finger feels heavy and restless, so I pull the trigger.

Luca screams. I want to say that we're laughing about this together but we're not. I'm just happy he'll never be able to use that slimy dick stick on anybody else ever again.

After a few seconds of him screaming, he spits out. "You fucking bitch, you will pay for this."

I probably will, I think to myself as I aim for an extremity and fire. I actually think I got his left foot but I'm not sure, he's howling in pain and flailing everywhere. I can't exactly tell, if the bitch would sit still for a second I would be able to see.

"I'm gonna kill everyone you've ever loved and make you watch," he grunts out, blood and spit flying from his mouth. How weird, well I guess the shot in the dick would make him hemorrhage. I'm beyond ignoring him now, his voice makes me cringe in disgust.

"Your parents begged me for mercy, but I'm gonna show you none." Luca starts saying this about my parents. "Your mom was the best lay I ever had." Okay, now it's getting ridiculous. For one, my mom could never stand him, she actually cringed when he was in the room.

"Sure buddy," I say as I pop off another shot trying to hit the same place in the shoulder he got me. *It's only fair, right?*

"Please stop." I do freeze for a second, Luca's voice is scared and almost childlike. This is the only time I've actually heard him sound like a human. With feelings and shit like that.

I smile at him as I aim the gun for his head. I'm standing right fucking next to him. He doesn't have the strength in his extremities anymore to take the gun away from me.

Maybe this is what I needed, or is this just gonna

fuck me up later in life? I'll probably have to spend the rest of my living years in some heavily induced therapy. Maybe they'll just put me in a psych house.

I refocus my attention back on Luca and smile, aiming the gun precisely at his head letting the bite of the metal sink into his forehead, showing him what is yet to come.

"I win," I say as cheerfully as I can. My smile is big and sincere. I'm actually feeling pretty good about myself right now. Before Luca gets the chance to answer, I fire two shots right in his head.

Yeah, one would've been enough, but I've read too many books and seen too many movies where the bad guy comes back.

Right when it's done, a whole new onslaught of emotions take over. I can feel them coming at me from everywhere. I don't feel like such a bad ass anymore with the blood of so many people all over me.

I start to spit to get it out of my mouth, vomiting comes next. I wish there was a river or something nearby. I'm just feeling sick and disgusted. God, maybe I am going crazy.

The tears don't stop, they just keep rolling down as I give up and lay myself against the SUV, slowly sliding down until I hit the ground.

I know my blood loss is insane. Maybe I should've cauterized the wound or had one of the guards stitch me fast at the house but then I would've never kept up. If I did any of that, Luca would've gotten away.

The nausea in the darkness takes over fast. I feel like I just want to lay on my side for a little while, maybe if I sleep for ten or fifteen minutes I'll feel stronger and better enough to get back up and get out of here.

I try to glance at the Maserati because she still has to be ready for me to drive. I rammed into the SUV but I didn't total the car.

I can't even see a foot in front of me, everything is hazy.

"Soon," I say to nobody in particular. I just know that soon I'll be with everybody in this world that matters to me. I get to see my parents again.

A car comes rumbling up. I can hear the crunching of gravel from the tires but I still can't find it within my strength to see who it is. Footsteps stomp in a hurry running toward me. If I felt any better, I would prepare for a blow or at least try to cover myself up.

I'm just sitting here leaning against the truck with my legs straight out in front of me and my hands drop down to my sides with my palms up. I probably look a little like the *grudge girl* as my head is still down, and my eyes rise up to see who is coming.

"Avery," I can hear the screaming as somebody runs up and slides next to me on the gravel. "Oh God, hold on." Not exactly sure who it was, but if I had to make a guess, I would say Mac, from the sweet sound of his voice. Plus the feeling of comfort I get from him being around. It couldn't be anybody else, because they're all gone.

Inside, I feel the tears coming, but I don't know if that's the same outside, I can't feel anything outside anymore.

I smile as much as I can, my work is done. Luca is gone, and he will never be able to hurt another person or family in this world. I can finally fucking die in peace.

This time I welcome the dark, I actually fucking embrace it.

EPILOGUE

AVERY

3 Months Later

I absentmindedly rub my belly as I watch through the window. For the last few months we've been pushing hard, getting the Romano estate back up and running.

The air conditioning systems had to be ripped out. When Asher slammed the wooden post inside of them, he destroyed them. Him doing that saved a ton of lives. We're definitely not worried about replacing three air conditioning units. I think we can afford it.

What matters is I don't know if he was thinking about it at the time, but him doing that kept the drugs from seeping into the house continuously.

They had a couple chemical engineers come in and test the amount of drugs that were in the air as opposed to how much was in the air conditioning. This whole thing was done really fast. The previous chemical engineer, who died, didn't have enough time to come up with a good healthy and safe plan. Luca, Seth and all of his guards didn't give a shit.

We're just lucky, the engineer could've made it deadlier, not giving any of us a chance, especially the ones that were in the house at the time.

All I know is from what we've been told, and what they found, is if the drugs would've kept filtering through the system, most likely everybody in the house, even those currently unconscious, would eventually die. It's just too much for any normal system to handle.

Asher saved everybody's life and it ended up almost killing him in the process.

"Hey baby," he says as he stands behind me and wraps his arm around my stomach.

While I was in the hospital, they found out that I was eight weeks pregnant. Eight fucking weeks pregnant. I was hell-bent on ending the life of Luca, not even caring if mine was taken, too. I never would've done this if I'd known I was pregnant. I never would've went after Luca. There's a baby inside of me that is more important than my thirst for revenge.

I'm extremely grateful now, and I couldn't be happier that Luca is gone. If he wasn't, he would be an opposing threat to my child now. Thankfully, all of the Delano's are gone. The world has gotten rid of some very sick and twisted individuals.

I pull Asher's hands around me tighter, beyond ecstatic that he's still here with me. He was just released from the hospital a month ago. They had to rehabilitate everything. Both of his femurs were shattered. My guy has metal rods in both legs, but it doesn't slow him down.

Since the first day out of a coma, Asher has been working on rebuilding his strength. I feel like I want to say he's stronger, but that's not true, he'll always have a little bit of weakness in his legs from what the gunshots did to them.

The bullet practically destroyed him inside and out. Almost leaving him wheelchair-bound forever, but thankfully he was determined.

When Asher found out that he was going to be a father, he upped his game ten times over, wanting to be everything he could be before his son was born without being wheelchair-bound. Even if he was in a chair, he would still be a great father. He almost killed himself again, by going through so much pain rehabilitating.

Asher was lucky, he was young and physically fit to overcome this. If this happened at another point in our lives, he might not be here.

I chuckle a little, but not too loud, not wanting to explain to Asher my thoughts. He went from protective to psychotically protective. I have a tracking app on my phone, on freaking everything. I probably have one implanted in my body somewhere, I better not!

We lost close to fifty guards. Unfortunately most of these men were killed while they were still sleeping and not from bullet wounds or anything, from the drugs in the air, the gas.

There were a couple men inside that were shot while they were sleeping, they must've woken up. That's the only logical explanation I can come up with.

Thankfully Mac is fine. It still bothers him to this day because Vito was a father figure to him, he meant the world to him. He keeps running scenarios in his head. I don't know if he'll ever be the same, but he just wishes that he would've slept outside like he normally does with the other guards. He didn't want to be that far away from the house because of Luca.

We've all tried to help with his resolve, to help him get over this but it's something he's got to do on his own. It's a long grieving process for all of us. Each one of us have to deal with it differently. Mac's is one of guilt and revenge. I stole the revenge, and I'm not giving that back.

"Asher," Carter yells from farther out in the grassy area. They set up a few practice football games to let off some steam. Asher bends down and gives me a kiss on the neck, then trails up to my cheek, finishing with my mouth, before he swats me in the ass and runs to play a game with his friends.

This is what I love seeing, this is what's comforting. Happiness and family. The back of my eyes burn as I fight the tears that keep slipping down. I miss Vito so much. A lot of people do. Thousands were at his funeral paying respect. Other Mafia bosses were there somewhat saddened and heartbroken. He didn't just keep us straightened out and doing well. He kept a lot of the families that way, too.

Even though he didn't run the East Coast, he was the head of the family meetings. The main decision-maker when it came to all things connected to the bosses.

The pain is excruciating and I know I'm not doing my baby any justice by being upset so much. I would never take away my time spent with Vito Romano, he was a wonderful man. Even though it hurts every fucking day and second, it was worth it.

I straighten my posture and rub my belly again as I look out and watch the guys play football. They're running and screaming at each other. They're also kind of brutal. At least they're not using guns and knives out there, shit can get messy, fast.

I watch Carter who seems to be a little bit down. My best friend Tate left for college a month ago. I pretty much had to kick her out of the fucking house. She didn't want to go, especially now that I'm pregnant. With everything that happened to us, she wanted to stay here and make sure that we're okay.

There's nothing here for her, I glance at Carter. Not sure of the whole story with them yet, but Tate's life is away at college being young and free. Not scared at every turn she makes, which is what she's done for almost two years. Not afraid anymore that her brothers are going to attack her.

Even though Armani is still out there, Asher has an idea of his location. I think he's waiting till the baby gets here, until he finishes his nephew once and for all.

Armani needs to fucking die, but at a different time when everything calms down. When the loss we've all experienced isn't so daunting anymore.

I smile as I watch Mac join the team. Even though morning sickness has been a bitch, we've been strategically working every day. Getting everything up to date and making sure Mac has what he needs so that he can run the Romano Empire, keeping the family name alive.

Mac will have to keep in correspondence with me at least several times a week, but I like it this way, so does Asher. My right-hand man is really excited to step up.

I do feel content and at peace as I rub the family crest on my thumb, it wouldn't fit anywhere else. I'm finally ready to start living the life that we deserve, one day at a time.

ABOUT THE AUTHOR

To keep in touch click below, or sign up for my News-
letter. Want more? Join my FB Reader Group.

ALSO BY K.J. THOMAS

Blackwood Academy

Hiding From Monsters

Running From Monsters

Taming the Monster

Moretti Siblings

Twisted Obsession

Cruel Obsession

ACKNOWLEDGMENTS

I want to sincerely let my Husband, kids and Nana know how much I appreciate them, not for what they've done during my writing of these books, but what they've endured. I was 100% book focused and nothing else. I love you guys!